For Angela,
With warm affection,
Car...

G000146936

Best
Friends
Tell
the
Best
Lies

Best Friends Tell the Best Lies

CAROL
DINES

**Delacorte
Press**

Published by
Delacorte Press
Bantam Doubleday Dell Publishing Group, Inc.
666 Fifth Avenue
New York, New York 10103

Copyright © 1989 by Carol Dines

All rights reserved.
No part of this book may be reproduced or transmitted
in any form or by any means, electronic or mechanical,
including photocopying, recording or by any information
storage and retrieval system, without the written permission
of the Publisher, except where permitted by law.

The trademark Delacorte Press ® is registered
in the U.S. Patent and Trademark Office.

Library of Congress Cataloging in Publication Data

Dines, Carol.
Best friends tell the best lies / Carol Dines.
    p.   cm.
Summary: Fourteen-year-old Leah's loyalty and devotion
to her emotionally troubled friend, Tamara, brings into
focus some of her conflicting feelings about her mother's
imminent remarriage and her own growing attachment to
a young Mexican American, the nephew of her
mother's boyfriend.
    ISBN 0-385-29704-1
    [1. Friendship—Fiction.   2. Emotional problems—Fiction.
3. Prejudices—Fiction.   4. Mothers and daughters—Fiction.
5. Mexican Americans—Fiction.]   I. Title.
PZ7.D6119Be   1989
[Fic]—dc19   88-29433
                                                        CIP
                                                         AC

Designed by Andrew Roberts

Manufactured in the United States of America

April 1989

10 9 8 7 6 5 4 3 2 1

BG

For Jack

The author wishes to acknowledge
and thank the Wisconsin Arts Board
for its support of this novel.

Best
Friends
Tell
the
Best
Lies

1

Tamara told me her mother's a murderer. At first I didn't believe her. I thought maybe Tamara was just trying to shock me, but then she started explaining the facts. You see, Tamara's had three stepfathers. Her real dad died in an automobile accident when she was only two years old. And the other men have all been old and rich.

"That's no coincidence!" Tamara whispered.

Tamara sits across from me in study hall. I had never seen her before the first day of school, but I sat next to her because her name's Luchio, mine's Lucas—we sit alphabetically. Right away I liked her because on the first day we were the only two girls who didn't wear makeup.

"My mother says it's only cheap girls who wear it at my age," Tamara whispered. "But she wears gobs. She's such a hypocrite, and she's a murderer!" That's when Tamara told me, "She's got a new victim too."

"I can't wear makeup either," I told her. "Mom says women wear it just to please men."

"Does she wear it?" Tamara asked.

I shook my head. "Just Moon Drops, wrinkle cream."

Then Tamara leaned toward me. "Mother's making a big mistake this time. Leonard's not as ancient as the others, and he's a lawyer. She'll get caught, I know it." Tamara paused and glanced around, like she was afraid someone else might be listening. "The others were practically senile when she married them, but Leonard's younger. He'll catch on and put her in prison. Then I'll get to throw great parties in our apartment."

There are two things you notice right away about Tamara—one is that she talks really fast, and the other is that Tamara looks much older than fourteen.

The first time I went to Tamara's condominium, I was scared to meet her mother. I had already met Tamara's older brother, Jake, who is totally opposite from Tamara. "He's a high-on," she said, "totally high on himself. All he thinks about is the basketball team. It's like he's in love with a basketball, nothing else counts."

She also told me her mother's a sorceress. I wasn't too sure what that meant, so I looked it up in the dictionary, which said a sorceress is a female wizard. Tamara said her mother reads all day, mainly books on herbs and natural foods. She also said her mother goes out and finds men who have had heart attacks, and then makes them fall in love with her. "That's how she makes a living, she finds dying men with large life-insurance policies. Then she speeds up the process."

Tamara nodded slowly. "She cooks all their food in butter and oil and tells her victims she's making special meals, stuff without fat. Then she does the opposite."

"Can't the doctors tell?"

"She can wrap anyone around her finger." Tamara sighed. "She's beautiful. She's one of the most beautiful women in the world. She could have been Miss America 1967, but she married my father instead."

"How does she stay so beautiful?" I asked.

"She plasters avocado on her face and puts cucumbers over her eyes. And she only eats red meat at other people's homes."

When we got to Tamara's building, one of the highest in Milwaukee, I realized they must have a lot of money—they own a whole floor overlooking Lake Michigan. "We knocked out some walls," Tamara said. "Bette's got a thing about space."

Inside everything was modern, totally opposite from where I live. The living room was all white, white chairs, white carpet, white pillows, except for this black marble square right in the middle of the room, but even that had a white vase with white silk flowers. And there were windows overlooking the city. We could even see the steeple of the church right down the block from where I live. But what I noticed most was how quiet it felt, I guess because we were up so high, on the fourteenth floor.

"Look," Tamara said, and she pointed to a whole wall of books with titles like *Eat Better, Feel Better* and *Vitamins: Your Key to Feeling Young.* "She finds out how people stay healthy and then she does the opposite." Tamara

3

stopped and looked at me. "I know you don't believe me, but wait until you see the kitchen!"

It was the biggest room in the house, with a long counter and copper pots hanging from the ceiling. Tamara began opening cabinets. "Look!" She pointed to bottles of oil—olive, corn, sesame, sunflower, peanut. Then she opened the refrigerator and pulled out one of the drawers "See?" She took out two sticks of butter. "Do you see margarine?"

Then she shook her head again. "This is the biggie, look!" She opened a whole cupboard lined with jars of nuts —pecans, cashews, walnuts, pistachios, hazelnuts. "Solid fat, the worst they can eat." Tamara stared at me. "I know you think I'm just saying all this, but wait and see. Poor Leonard."

Suddenly we heard a key in the front door. Tamara smiled and nodded slowly. "Just wait—don't let appearances fool you." I'd prepared myself to meet a real sorceress, someone who dressed in black and looked mysterious, but then I was face-to-face with Tamara's mom, who came in smiling, and said, "Hi, honey," and handed the grocery bag to Tamara.

"Bette, this is Leah, Leah, this is my mother, Bette."

I couldn't believe Tamara called her mother by her first name. My mom would've killed me.

Mrs. Luchio was totally opposite from what I had expected. What surprised me most about her was that she wore really normal clothes, just a denim skirt with a turtleneck sweater and boots. She was beautiful, with black hair, braided and wrapped around her head. Her skin was white, which seemed strange because everything else about her was dark. Dark eyes, dark eyebrows and eyelashes. Even her lips were a dark red.

"Would you girls like a snack?" Mrs. Luchio asked.

"No, thanks, Bette, we've already helped ourselves." Tamara grabbed my arm and pulled me toward the hallway. "See?" she whispered. "She controls with food."

Tamara kept tugging my sleeve. I turned to say good-bye to Mrs. Luchio. I felt embarrassed, walking out of the room while she was still speaking. "I'm so glad to meet you, Leah. Tamara rarely invites her friends over—she likes to keep her life private."

I wondered if Mrs. Luchio knew how Tamara talked about her—I found it hard to believe someone so pretty could be a murderer.

"Leonard's coming for dinner, honey. Maybe Leah would like to stay too?"

I would have liked to, but Tamara spoke quickly. "No, she has to get home. She just came over to see my fish."

"Thank you anyway," I said, and turned because Tamara was jerking my arm practically out of its socket.

She had the best bedroom I've ever seen, all blues and greens. Her water bed had a huge green spread, and when we lay on our backs, we bobbed a little before it settled. "Normally these beds aren't allowed, but Mom paid off the management, otherwise I wouldn't have moved here."

Tamara also had a huge aquarium with live fish. The guppy swam in a stabbing motion but the other fish just settled into one spot, so I got bored watching. Before I left, Tamara pulled out this nylon bag she had in her purse. Inside were bottles and tubes of makeup. "Mom threw these out," she whispered. "So meet me in the bathroom before class, and we can look normal for once."

That's how Tamara and I became best friends. I'd meet her in school every morning, and we'd put on makeup. I'd do her, and she'd do me, but the best part was hearing about

5

Mrs. Luchio. "Bette served chicken last night, with cream sauce, can you believe it? And potatoes with sour cream, and asparagus with hollandaise! I mean, Leonard would have to be crazy not to see through her."

"Did he eat it?"

"Of course. He doesn't suspect a thing, yet!"

When I told Mom about Tamara's mother being a murderer, she wouldn't believe it. She thought Tamara was only kidding. But when I told her that Tamara was serious, she said Tamara sounded disturbed. "I'd like to meet your friend," Mom said. "It sounds like maybe she should see one of the counselors at your school."

"But why else would Mrs. Luchio marry three very old, very sick men?" I asked. "And why did they just happen to be rich?" I paused to see if Mom was listening. "That's not a coincidence!" I added, just like Tamara had told me.

2

Ever since José and Mom started dating, she and I have been fighting a lot. It's like I can't control it. I mean, I don't understand how Mom got attracted to José in the first place. He's okay, but nothing special. Mom says stuff like he's got both feet on the ground, and his head's on solid, but I think Mom was alone too long before she met him. The truth is, José's fat. Nice, maybe, but fat.

When José was first hired as vice-principal at Tech High, where Mom's a social worker, I thought they liked each other because they worked well together. I never thought Mom could get serious about him. But then, when José was supposed to be promoted to principal, and instead got passed over because the superintendent hired someone from outside, Mom got really upset.

"If he weren't Mexican, they would have promoted him." Mom said. "He doesn't fit their image of a principal, that's the real reason he didn't get promoted."

That's when she started spending a lot of time with José and convinced him to file a lawsuit against the school superintendent's office. And that's when I realized that Mom liked him better than just a friend.

Even before I met José, Mom talked to me about her doubts. "He keeps asking me out, but I don't know if I should date someone from work. What if we have an argument and I have to sit with him the next day at a committee meeting?"

I wasn't really taking Mom's dilemma seriously, partly because I hadn't met José yet. I pictured a totally different kind of man, basically the tall, dark, and handsome type.

"I'd go for it. You're not getting any younger," I told her. "Just make sure he can afford to buy us a house if you two get serious."

Mom smiled. "I really respect him—not just how he acts toward me, but the changes he's brought about at the school. The kids like him too."

"Changes?" I asked.

"He listens when the kids go in to talk to him. He doesn't automatically side with the teachers, he hears everyone's side. I like that."

Usually Mom doesn't get worked up over having guests for dinner, but the night José was invited over to meet me, she set the table three different ways before she settled on candles and a checked tablecloth. "He's more the informal type," she said.

Mom normally comes home, puts on her blue jeans, and pins her red hair on top of her head while she cooks dinner. But the day José came over, she wore her hair long. And even though Mom almost never wears makeup, she put on a little blush and eyebrow pencil. Plus, she wore her red silk blouse and black pants that show off her body, which is pretty decent considering she's thirty-four and her only exercise is gardening.

"Ooh." I clicked my tongue. "Very sexy, aren't we?"

"Well, he is my boss!" Mom looked down at herself and paused. "Do you think I'm too dressed up?"

"Why are you so worried? You see him every day, right? I mean, you probably just saw him less than two hours ago, correct?" I stood next to her. "So are you two going to make out after dinner? I mean, should I leave the living room and slam my bedroom door shut so he knows you're alone? Should I make tons of noise if I go to the bathroom so you can pull your clothes back on?"

Mom blushed and shook her head. "He's coming over so he can meet you. I've told him all about my wonderful daughter."

I smiled; but it was the last time I felt like smiling the entire evening, basically because the minute José arrived I went into shock. Mom had said he was pleasantly plump, but if that's the case, love is definitely, and I mean definitely, blind.

The first thing he did was hand her flowers and kiss her on the lips, with his hands on her bottom. I mean, spread across her bottom. "You look beautiful," he whispered, right in front of me. I mean, what was I supposed to do, lift his hand off her bottom and shake it?

"José, this is Leah. Leah, this is José."

"Well, it's about time," José stated. "I had to force your mom to invite me for dinner. It's taken me since July—three months—to get an invitation."

9

"She's a very popular woman," I said, hoping to discourage him.

Mom laughed, as if I'd just cracked the biggest joke of the century.

I couldn't picture it—Mom with José. He wore shiny shirts that opened halfway down his chest, like he was showing off his hair. And you could see his fat roll where the shirt creased. And when he laughed, which was often, his whole stomach jiggled. No wonder he didn't get promoted to principal!

During the evening he kept bringing the conversation back to Mom, heaping the compliments on top of each other. *It's clear why she likes him,* I thought, *he's one constant ego boost.*

"Your mother's the best counselor I've ever seen. She should be teaching social work at the university, training other people, you know?"

I nodded. The entire evening I agreed with everything he said. I figured it was best to be agreeable and get him out of there as soon as possible so Mom and I could have a good, long talk about her future.

"So," Mom said, as soon as he left, "what do you think?"

"I think you can do a lot better!"

Mom stared at me and shook her head. "Well, then, tell me what kind of man you think I should choose."

"Rich," I said. "Handsome. Smart. Someone with a good sense of humor."

"That's exactly how I see José," Mom replied. "Except for the rich part."

"Don't you think you could find someone a little more your type, Mom?" I asked. "I mean, there are lots of men around, right?"

"I'm not in the market for Mr. Perfect, Leah. José's got a lot to offer."

"If you're going by bulk weight." It was a mean thing to say, but I meant it. That's how I felt, like Mom was making a big mistake, and if she got stuck with him, I would too.

Mom glared at the dishes in the sink, then whispered, "Leah, tell me the truth. Why don't you like him?"

"He's okay, Mom. I don't dislike him. It's just the way he looks. I mean, those clothes and his hair, all greased back and everything. I picture you with someone else. . . . You know, a head-turner like Dad."

Mom stared at me. "I really like José. A lot!" And before I could say anything, she changed the subject by telling me we were all invited to the Spencers' party.

"Who's all?"

"You, me, and José."

"I'm not going to the Spencers' party," I told her. "No way."

"Because you're a snob?" Mom smiled. "And you don't want to be seen with someone who looks a little different from yourself?"

Mom stared with her big eyes like she knew exactly what I was thinking. And I didn't care if she was right, there's no way I'd go to a party with Mom and José. Especially since he's always patting Mom's bottom and holding her hand. No way. "Why is everything supposed to revolve around you?" I asked her.

"You and Rachel Spencer used to be good friends."

"Right, Mom. Used to be." I thought about telling Mom what Rachel had said after I had shown her this really handsome picture of Dad. "No wonder he divorced your mom," Rachel had said with a laugh. That was after she had practically gone into shock because I'd told her we

11

don't have a subscription to *The New York Times.* "What do your parents read?" she'd asked, and then, like she had made this huge mistake, she goes, "I mean parent, what does your mother read?"

That's Rachel's way, aim right for the throat.

But I don't tell Mom stuff like that. In fact, since José's been spending time with Mom, I don't tell her anything. Whenever I look at her, I see how much she's changed. For one thing, she's gotten fatter in the last month, which proves José's not a good influence. Last night, for example. José brought over this bag of fried chicken, cole slaw, biscuits, and ice cream.

"Special for the ladies," he said, like it was some big banquet. "So you won't have to lift a finger. I'll even do the dishes." Then he looked at me. "It's all here, no one has to cook a thing."

I don't know what got into me, but my voice came out all wrong. "Mmm. Just what you need—more grease!"

It was that kind of moment when you know you've hurt somebody, but to say anything else would only make things worse. I laughed, hoping he'd think it was a joke, but it was too late. Mom's face was bright red, and she was about to yell at me, when José spoke. "I'm terribly sorry fried chicken offends you," he said, his voice overly polite. "Perhaps you can suggest a place nearby where I can go next time?"

Okay, so now Mom is fat and happy and I shouldn't deny her happiness, I know, but she shouldn't expect me to treat José like my father. I sat there watching them eat four pieces each. José kept passing me the white meat. "Take it now, or there won't be any left," he warned, laughing like it was great to be a glutton. I tried to be polite, but all I could see was how Mom was making a big mistake.

12

She pretends that since José's been dropping by, nothing's changed. She pretends that the differences between them don't exist. I mean, it's not like Rachel's parents, who are both doctors. It's easy to hang out at her house. There, we can be private. Not here. Not with José humming all over the house and Mom using the kitchen to do her students' evaluations.

I can just see bringing Rachel over here and having José and Mom stuff their faces, talking all the time. Rachel would say something mean like "I didn't know your mom brought her work home. Is she researching bilingual weight-control programs?"

And I'd just laugh, because what else could I do?

3

What amazes me about Tamara is that she doesn't care what other people think of her. "Most people only use ten percent of their brains anyway, so why worry?" she asked me. That's the thing about Tamara, she's very convincing.

A few days ago she came to my locker before first hour, and when I looked up, I almost didn't recognize her. "Tamara!" She had cut her hair short so the top stood straight up with spikes for sideburns. Under her black stretch pants she had white lace stockings and high heels, which she said she'd borrowed "unnoticed" from Bette. Over that she wore this long man's shirt with a chain hanging around her hips, an honest-to-God chain, padlock and all, the kind people use to lock their bikes.

"What do you think?" She smiled, then straightened her tie. "This belonged to Saul, my mother's last victim."

"You look like the victim," I teased her.

Tamara pulled out a magazine photo with a picture of celebrities at the Cannes Film Festival toasting champagne glasses. "What do you think?" Tamara asked, shaking the picture in my face.

She actually looked like them—I mean, the hair and clothes, anyway.

"Look," Tamara whispered, "if my mother kills Leonard, I'm not sticking around a day longer. I'm heading to California, and I'm not going to arrive with Milwaukee written all over me. Plus," and she smiled so her teeth looked really white next to the purple lipstick, "I need some practice."

"Practice at what?"

"Looking interesting—that's what counts. It's all style, the image one projects." Tamara turned around so I could get a full view. "I should know! Style is the only reason people like Bette—what else is there to like?" She pressed her lips together. "I'm practicing for California. You can't just arrive and be famous, it takes experience to be a good actress."

As I looked at Tamara walk down the hallway, her chain slanting over her hips, I kept thinking about what people would say. I could never dress like that. I guess I'm too much like Mom. I remember last Christmas, when Mom put on a new dress that Grandma Lucas had sent her. I kept seeing her walk past the hallway mirror, like she was worried her slip was showing. "I feel so weird in a dress, Leah. Everyone's going to think I'm after my professor."

"So don't wear it, then."

15

"Everybody's so used to seeing me in jeans, I'm actually embarrassed to dress up, isn't that stupid?"

"You're too old to worry about what people think of you," I said, repeating exactly what she always said to me.

When Mom got home that night, I asked her how it had gone. "Did you get hassled about your dress?"

Suddenly Mom's chin crumpled as she put her head down on the kitchen table and started to cry. She looked up and rubbed her nose. Then she started laughing really hard, too hard considering nothing funny had been said. "Nobody said anything," she whispered. "No one even noticed."

That's the way Mom was before she met José. She'd say one thing in the morning, something else at night. Her moods were constantly changing. I used to tease her and say, "Mom, do you know what time of day it is?" That was our code, my way of telling her she was acting weird again. And she'd check her watch and say, "It's time." And I'd nod, which meant it was time for her to shape up. I guess, when you're close to someone, you need codes, a nice way of saying what you don't like about that person.

Like Tamara and me. We have a code for the cheerleaders. We call them the canaries, because they have chirpy voices. Then there are the people who join the clubs, they're the addicts, all addicted to each other. When we see them, we make this motion like we're shooting up. The guys we don't like, we call them the singles, and the guys who are okay, we call them the Quarter Pounders.

"But hold the onion," Tamara always says.

And then I go, "Hold the ketchup."

And then she says, "Lots of mayonnaise," which is gross, but Tamara enjoys being gross when we're alone.

Tamara likes this guy named Caesar. I figured that out the other day when she wanted to stand at this certain place

16

near the boys' bathroom. These three guys came out smelling like cigarette smoke, and Tamara whispered, "Quarter Pounder." Caesar was the one in the middle with black boots, a blue-jean jacket, and his hair cut short, flat-topped.

Tamara started walking right behind him. "Quarter Pounder," she whispered again.

"All bun," I told her, meaning there's nothing inside.

That's when she stopped and pulled me over to the side of the hallway. She started telling me all about him—everything, his schedule, his locker number, even his favorite sport, which is judo. I was amazed. I guess that's one of the advantages of having an older brother like Jake who can tell Tamara about all the guys in his class.

Anyway, the next day Tamara wore her chain and padlock again. She told me she was going to hand Caesar the key to the lock. Only later, I saw her looking depressed outside the cafeteria. "He's not here today, no Quarter Pounder."

I grabbed the key and threatened to give it to Ronny Tandersen, the biggest computer nerd at our school, who tutors us sometimes in computer class.

"Go ahead." Tamara laughed. "He wouldn't know what to do with it. Poor Ronny can't see beyond his own hardware!"

4

When I told Tamara about Rachel Spencer's party, she told me I shouldn't worry about what people think of Mom and José. "If they're renting a disc jockey, I'd go. You'll meet some guys!" Tamara always talks about guys, usually about her mother's boyfriends.

"Why do you care what Rachel Spencer thinks?" Tamara asked. "She sounds like a very tedious person." Tamara's been using the word *tedious* a lot lately. She says her teachers are tedious, Bette's haircut is tedious, her brother's friends are tedious. It's one of her word kicks. Last week everything was "regrettable."

"If you worry about Rachel Spencer, you're tedious," Tamara stated.

That's when I told her how I really felt about Mom and

José's relationship. "I can't stand how she acts around him. She pretends he's perfect."

"Mothers are like that, they expect you to go along with whatever they want. It's like the older their kids get, the more mothers mutate . . . the less human they become. Like if you happen to enjoy wearing black three days in a row," Tamara added, "your mother writes a law against wearing black. And if you kiss a guy, your mother can smell his saliva from a mile away."

"Does saliva have an odor?" I asked.

"To mothers it does. Although they don't seem to notice it in the morning when their boyfriends sleep over."

Sometimes it seemed like Tamara was part of a much larger, more interesting world than I had ever known existed—and she was teaching me all about it. "Bette's boyfriends stay over?" I asked.

"Her victims." Tamara nodded. "And mothers are geniuses when it comes to remembering . . . especially when it comes to remembering how simple things were when they were your age. How easy they were compared to you."

I listened, nodding.

"And they're mathematically brilliant when it comes to subtracting their lives from yours, like when you need a ride someplace, and suddenly they start computing all the rides they've given you in the last seven years. But the worst," Tamara whispered, her eyes growing wide, "is that mothers kill their young . . . if they're weak."

"Tamara!" I groaned. Sometimes her imagination got too weird.

"Well, sometimes I feel like Bette gnaws away at me. Like all her questions are swallowing me."

"Yeah." That I could relate to.

19

"It's like they think they have a right to know everything."

I nodded.

Tamara's expression suddenly turned serious. "You have to promise something. You have to swear you'll never tell anyone what we talk about. No one."

"Shake on it." I stuck out my hand.

"You watch too much TV." Tamara rolled her eyes. "I'll take your word for it."

Then she glanced around the hallway, to make sure no other students were nearby. "See, Bette doesn't fall in love, she's incapable of it, so it never hurts to try to destroy her relationships. But if your mom and José are in love, it makes it harder to ruin their feelings for each other."

Tamara's voice was matter-of-fact, as if we were discussing a homework assignment.

"Do you think they'll get married?" Tamara asked.

I shrugged. "Not for a while. Mom always says she doesn't want to repeat her past mistakes. Meaning Dad. She says she'll never be dependent on someone else for something she can do herself."

"God, that's the absolute opposite from Bette. She says, never do something for yourself when you can get someone else to do it for you."

"See, with Dad, Mom didn't work. And then when they got a divorce, Mom had to get a job, which was hard because she hadn't been to college, and school costs her a lot of money, which is why we still don't even own a house." I felt embarrassed admitting that to Tamara, but I figured she'd find out sooner or later.

"Sounds like your mom could take lessons from Bette. She inherited a bundle from her father, so she's never

20

worked, especially since she's killed off her exes. Life-insurance policies bring in a nice income."

"Wait until you see José. It's hard to believe Mom could love him."

Tamara nodded. "Does he sleep over?"

"No, not while I'm there. Though once when I got home from visiting Grandma Lucas, there was a book of his lying on the bed. I asked Mom if he'd stayed over."

"What'd she say?"

"She said it was none of my business."

Tamara nodded like she understood. "That's how mothers are when they fall in love—they act as if their lovelife has absolutely nothing to do with you. Like Bette. She pretends that I'm too young to understand she's making a mint off male senior citizens. One thing's for sure . . . if Leonard goes, then I go too."

Tamara leaned close to me and whispered. "You could end their relationship, you know, if you wanted to."

"What?"

"You know, pour a little cold water on the fire, extinguish it."

"How?"

She paused and smiled. "I've got an idea."

I hesitated. "What kind of idea?"

"An idea that will protect your mom from making the biggest mistake of all—marrying José. He's already changed her, right?"

"She's gotten fatter," I whispered, without mentioning that she also seemed happier.

"This is what you have to ask yourself: Is this the man you want to come to your graduation? Is this the man you want to introduce to your dates? Don't you see, you have to do something now!"

21

"Okay. . . ." I said, wanting to be as adventurous as Tamara, because that's what I loved about her—she wasn't afraid to be herself.

"It won't make me feel too guilty, will it?"

"My shrink says guilt's a cover-up for anger," Tamara stated in a matter-of-fact way.

My mouth dropped open—she'd never mentioned a shrink before. She must have seen my shock, because then she rolled her eyes, like it was no big deal. "He's practically my father! Bette used to date him. He was one of the few who survived."

But before I could ask her about it, she changed the subject. "Does José have an accent? I love the way Spanish men talk—they're supposed to be great kissers."

"No," I told her. "He talks like you and me. He's not even really Spanish. He was born in California, but his parents are from Mexico."

"Where in California?"

"L.A."

"Really?" Tamara sat up. "If he knows L.A., then he must know Hollywood, so he can fill me in."

That made me mad. She wasn't supposed to like José. I stared at her without saying anything, so she'd get the message.

"Well?" Tamara asked. "Are you going to save your mom from her own nightmare?"

I nodded.

"Then meet me here tomorrow, after school."

The next afternoon I hurried to the intersection in front of the drugstore, where I could see Tamara walking toward me up the hill, carrying a huge brown bag.

"Okay, this is what you do. You wait until your mom has José over, but you pick a time when she's tired and doesn't look very good. You know, like before dinner some night when she's just gotten home from work. Does José sometimes come over then?"

"He comes over a lot for dinner."

"Okay, so you stay in your room until your mother calls you. Then when she calls you, you don't come out, not at first."

"Why not?"

"You wait until she comes to get you, or better yet, you wait until José comes to get you, if she sends him."

Tamara paused, smiling, like she was waiting for a response.

"Yeah?" I asked.

"And you wear this. You pretend not to notice what you're wearing and you ask José, right in front of your mom, if he can help you with your homework. Make sure he has to lean over your shoulder so he can see down your front."

Tamara giggled. "And make sure you pick a really difficult problem, like in math or chemistry, so he has to help you for a while. See, your mom will grow crazy watching him watch you. Believe me, you'll see a lot less of Mr. Margarita after that."

I had my doubts. "What if it doesn't work?"

"Well, to make sure it works . . . the next time he's over, you wait until he's leaving to go someplace, then you ask him for a ride. You have to be really nice and polite about it. Then, when he drops you off, you wait awhile before you go home. Your mom will go crazy—guaranteed."

23

Tamara handed me the bag. I looked inside and couldn't believe it. Mom would die.

"No way, Tamara, I can't wear this."

"Let's go try it on before you say another word," she insisted.

We went back to Tamara's place, where I put on the black silk shirt with lace that barely covered my chest. As I stared at the mirror, I was shocked. You could see through the silky material.

"It's a maillot," Tamara told me, "Bette's got tons of tops like that. There's a shirt that goes on top, but I can't find it."

"Tamara, I can't wear this without something on top."

"Why not?"

"It's like wearing nothing."

"Exactly. There's a skirt to match, just make sure the slit is on the side. And here are the underpants."

"They're black! I can't wear black underpants."

"Nobody's going to see them—it's so your underwear won't show through the skirt. They have to be the same color as the skirt."

Amazed, I held the small strip of black in front of the light. "When does Bette wear these?"

"When her victims begin to get suspicious." Tamara sighed deeply. "She wears this kind of outfit just as the men begin their decline, when they start losing their appetites for her cooking."

"Won't your mom notice the clothes are missing?"

"Leonard's away, so she won't need them." Tamara handed me the bag. "Men go crazy when they see women in black."

5

The next day I did everything just as Tamara had suggested. "Put your hair on top of your head, so you show off your neck and your chest . . . very important." Tamara had explained everything. "Wear some jewelry and perfume, but not too much. You don't want to overdo it. You just want your mom to know she's got some heavy-duty competition. Wear lipstick too. And eyeliner. You need some dark stuff to make you look older. But no mascara. It smudges. Just eyeliner."

Once I was dressed, I sat and looked at myself. No way could I go through with it. I called Tamara at home and told her it was too weird.

"Then don't do it," she stated, her voice cold.

"It's too obvious. Mom'll know right away what's up."

"So . . . you want her to know. You want both of them to know how desperate you are." Tamara sighed. "Don't be passive!"

"Tamara, what does this prove?"

"It proves you're not a little girl whose mother can tell you how to run your life. José definitely has an effect on you. Right? So you're taking matters into your own hands. Your reflecting your mother's own behavior."

"Tamara, my mother would never dress like this."

"You'll expose José's lust for women. All Latin men have it, you know. And if Mom's seventy-year-old boy-friends like it, think what it'll do to José! You're saving your mom from a grave mistake."

"José doesn't seem like the type to go for this—"

"Trust me. All men are the type. The worst that can happen is that you leave the room and change your clothes, right? Look at it as an experiment."

"I don't know."

"Look, I went to a lot of trouble to help you. I got you the clothes and the makeup and told you how to do every-thing . . . all you have to do is carry it out, for a few minutes at least. That's all." Tamara sounded impatient. "Promise you'll at least try?"

"Okay," I whispered, and then she hung up before I could change my mind. What a difference clothes and makeup make. I mean, I looked really different—I looked older, for one thing, and for another, I looked sexy, which was something I normally wasn't too sure of. I concentrated on how Tamara would act—I wished I was more like her—she seemed to know exactly what she wanted and how to get it.

I waited in my room, with my books sprawled out on

my bed, my skirt slung open so my panties were visible. Very sexy, I thought. Tamara should see me now!

Mom and José were in the kitchen. I could smell mushrooms frying, which most likely meant an omelette, José's so-called specialty.

It wouldn't be long.

"Leah . . ."

Finally.

"Leah! Dinner's ready." Mom yelled louder. "Leah, come now while it's hot."

You come, while I'm hot, I thought. With Tamara's clothes and makeup I felt like a different person . . . more powerful. Like Tamara must feel with the chain and padlock wrapped around her hips.

Suddenly the door opened, and Mom stood there, staring, her eyes wide. "Dinner is . . ." She paused. "Why are you dressed like that? Where did those clothes come from?"

"I bought them—and I'm wearing them because they're comfortable." Then, just like Tamara had told me, I got up quickly and moved into the kitchen before Mom could say anything about changing my clothes.

"Hi, José." I smiled at him. "How are you?"

He was putting everything on the table, and when he saw me, he stopped and stared. He looked at Mom as if he didn't know what to say, but Mom only shrugged and continued staring at me as if she could steam a message into my brain—obviously she wanted me to know she was mad!

"Where are you going tonight?" José asked. "You look dressed up."

"Yes," Mom said sarcastically. "All dressed up just for our benefit."

"Why not?" I said casually. "José's our guest," and I smiled at him again.

27

That made Mom angrier, and Mom's not one to hide her emotions. She ate silently, glancing at me while she chewed her food. Once, when our eyes met, she shook her head and rolled her eyes, as if to say she'd never understand me.

I picked at my dinner, feeling too excited to really eat. I liked getting people's attention by dressing this way. Suddenly I found myself asking José all kinds of questions I'd never considered asking before, like how old he was, and why had he become a vice-principal instead of teaching history, like he used to.

José kept looking at me too—all of me, like he couldn't quite believe it was me. Then he'd look at Mom, hoping to catch her eye, but the only time Mom looked at him, she just stared, without cracking the slightest smile.

"So what's new with you?" he finally asked as if he wanted to find out why I was so dressed up.

"Not much. . . ." I paused. "Except, I'm flunking out of chemistry. We have a test tomorrow and I just can't seem to get one of the problems. Could you help me after dinner?"

He glanced first at Mom, who put down her fork and stared back at him, like she was waiting for his answer.

"I should help your mom do the dishes."

"I'll do the dishes later, if you help me do my homework." I looked at José, raising my eyebrows, urgently. "If you don't help me I might really flunk. And Mom's terrible at science."

"It's up to your mom," José said.

Mom looked at me, up and down. "Is this necessary?" she asked.

Tamara had told me to play dumb no matter what, so I looked at Mom and smiled. "Is what necessary?"

"This game!"

"I don't consider my homework a game. I thought you'd be glad if I asked José to help me. You're always talking about how great he is at everything." I sent José another big smile.

Mom looked ready to explode. She shrugged her shoulders, and nodded toward José. "Fourteen going on thirty . . . thanks to her new best friend."

My face turned hot. "If José doesn't help me, I'm going to flunk. I don't understand the equations."

José nodded, looking at his food. "Okay, if your mother says it's all right."

I giggled. "Why wouldn't she say it was all right? I mean, she's always after me to do better in chemistry, and now I have a personal tutor. It's okay with you, isn't it, Mom?"

Mom's face was bright red, so I knew I'd better cool it. "Sure," she said. "Why not?" Her eyes rested on José.

"Let's get started." I led José back to my room. I scooted backward on my bed so my skirt opened, and I saw José's eyes follow my leg, upward. He sat down on the edge of the bed and picked up my book. "Okay," he whispered, "show me the problem."

I couldn't believe what happened next. Mom brought José a cup of coffee and sat down next to him, watching us. She sat there the entire time, pretending to be interested in my chemistry.

José always comes over for a few minutes after school to have a cup of coffee with Mom, and often he stays for dinner. But Wednesdays he leaves early to go downtown for the school board meeting, so the next afternoon I asked him for a ride. "I just need a lift to the library, okay?"

José smiled. "It's up to your mom."

Mom glared at me. "You'll be home before dark?"

I nodded and grabbed my coat. "Don't worry, Mom, I can take care of myself."

I called Tamara from the library. "Mom seems madder at me than at José. I don't know if she'll stop seeing him just because she's jealous."

"What about José?"

"He doesn't really seem any different than usual."

"Then move to plan B. Cling to them. Never give them a minute to themselves. After a while they'll start to fight."

When I got home just before dinner, Mom ignored me. She waited until dinner to ask me how my chemistry test went, and when I replied that I'd done well, thanks to José, she started shaking her head.

"It won't work, Leah."

"What won't work?" I asked.

"I'll just say this once. Stop trying to hurt me. You're making a fool out of yourself."

Then it happened. I started crying right in front of Mom, which ruined the whole scheme.

"Leah, I like José a lot, and you are not going to interfere."

"Who's interfering?" I sniffled. "I haven't done anything."

Usually when I cried, Mom was sympathetic, but not then. "Did Tamara give you those clothes? Did she put you up to this? Because if she did, I hope you'll find a new friend. I miss the old you. The way you used to be."

I left the room, whispering to myself, "I miss the old you too." And I said it just loud enough for Mom to hear.

6

I thought about Tamara's suggestion, spying on José and Mom, never giving them time to themselves, but they were always asking me to join them anyway. It wasn't like I'd have to spy to find out information—they were always volunteering information. Like last week, when José told Mom outright that he was invited to his old girlfriend's wedding.

"Am I invited too?" Mom had asked, winking at me.

"Of course." And José had leaned over and hugged Mom. "It's a good opportunity for you to see a Mexican wedding—there's lots for you to learn."

Mom shook her head. "Let's change the subject."

Now, what was I supposed to say to that?

José always teases Mom about marrying him, right in

front of me. A few days ago her car broke down, and José had to come all the way over from his apartment to find out why the engine wouldn't start.

"If we were married," José told her outright, as if he didn't care if I heard, "you wouldn't have to go through this —I'd make sure the radiator had water. . . . And I wouldn't have to drive across town at seven in the morning, I could just come out in my pajamas."

"True." Mom had said. "But—"

" 'But—' " José mimicked Mom's voice, " 'I don't want to get married until I finish graduate school because I don't want to repeat the same mistake.' " Then he poured water into the radiator and started the engine. "I love being defined as a potential mistake."

"You know that's not what I mean."

"A woman of principles!" His voice was sarcastic. "Someday you're going to realize that you're much more independent than you give yourself credit for—and that you can be independent and still love someone."

I watched as José slammed the hood shut.

"You see?" He laughed as he tapped the rim of the car and shook his head sadly. "It didn't hurt so much to call me and ask for help."

Mom smiled. "It didn't hurt because you came. I haven't always been so lucky."

So how am I supposed to spy when they discuss everything in front of me anyway? Plus, I don't think spying's such a good idea right now because Mom's already suspicious. She keeps telling me to bring Tamara over for dinner, and when I tell her Tamara's always busy, she gets this look on her face. I call it her know-it-all expression, like if she stares hard enough, she'll see what I'm thinking.

"You never used to be ashamed of me," Mom whispered

the other day. "And I know you're not narrow-minded enough to be ashamed of a man like José just because he's overweight."

"It's more than that," I mumbled. "He dresses—"

"I don't want to hear it, Leah. And if your friends won't accept someone like José, then maybe you need to reconsider who you're choosing for friends."

"It's easy for you to say, Mom. You married Dad and he was the handsomest guy around . . . and still is. You yourself even said everybody thought you were great because Dad was so good-looking."

"Leah, I married your father because he also had personality."

"Mom, I can't help it if I care about what people think! If José were my stepfather, everyone would think we were weird just because of the way he dresses."

"Is that why you won't go to the Spencers' party?" Mom asked.

I shrugged.

"Well, at least invite Tamara over so I can meet her. If it'll make any difference, have her over on a night when I'm going over to José's—that way I can meet her, but you won't have to introduce her to him. We can save that for another time."

I actually did ask Tamara over, for Friday night.

I figured I might as well risk showing her our apartment —if she didn't like me afterward, there was nothing I could do about it.

"Can't Friday." That's all she said, so I figured maybe it had something to do with her shrink.

It's easier anyway if we go over to Tamara's place, because we can be alone there. Bette usually goes out with Leonard. And before they go, they always ask us if we want to join them, but of course, Tamara always answers, "Sorry, we're busy." That's all she ever says.

"If you give in once," she told me, "they'll think they've got the best of you. I'll never go out with them. I won't have anything to do with Bette until she stops poisoning men!"

"Maybe you could warn Leonard!"

Tamara rolled her eyes. "Don't you think I already have, hundreds of times? I've told him about Saul, Richard, and Simon. I've already explained that they had strokes and they were all rich. Then I told him to watch what he eats when Mom cooks."

"And what did he say?"

"His mouth was full!" Tamara laughed. "It's something Bette does to men—they never question her. So I have to do it for them. See, Bette knows I see through her. Ever since Saul, I've known the truth."

"What truth?"

"She cares more about finding rich husbands than she cares about Jake and me."

"But she's so beautiful, she could have anybody."

"She says it's my fault she's not married. She says no man wants to take on a teenage daughter like me. But I know—she's just jealous of me, that I'm young and she's getting old—she views me as competition. Even my shrink says so."

"Why don't you come over and meet José—then you can give me suggestions."

"No way." Tamara shook her head. "Once your mother meets me, she'll turn you against me. I know, from experience."

*   *   *

34

I forgot to tell Mom I was going to Tamara's Friday after school, and when I got home, there was a note. *I'm at José's. Call me.*

The phone only rang once before she picked up the receiver. "Leah, we are going to have a long talk when I get home tonight. And you're grounded the rest of the weekend."

"Just for forgetting to tell you where I was going?" I couldn't believe it.

"It's eight-thirty on a Friday night, and I've been trying to reach you since three-thirty."

"I was at Tamara's."

"I'll be home by eleven, and if you're still up, we'll talk. Otherwise, tomorrow. I want to discuss Tamara with you."

I was in bed by the time I heard the engine of the car sputtering into the driveway. Mom opened my door as I lay with my eyes closed.

"Okay, then," Mom whispered, "we'll talk tomorrow morning."

"If you insist," I whispered back, just the way I imagined Tamara would say it, and then I added, "Jessica," my mother's name. "If you insist, Jessica!" I repeated, louder.

Mom slammed the door shut.

I lay there wide awake, listening to the silence that takes over our apartment at night, a silence that makes me feel separate from everyone. I used to go sleep with Mom when I felt that way, when the creaking and sputtering of the radiators was the only sound left in the whole world. But not anymore, I couldn't sleep with Mom now. She'd try to make me feel like a little girl again if I went into her room. That's what bothered me about Mom: either way, whether I needed her or not, she'd make me feel guilty.

35

7

Saturday morning Mom definitely wasn't in a good mood. "Sit down." She looked at me, then at the clock. "It's important that we straighten things out. I'm very concerned by the changes I've noticed in you."

"What changes?"

"Attitude changes."

"I haven't changed."

"You have, Leah. Ever since you met Tamara."

"How, then?" I wanted proof.

"Little things. I see the makeup left over on your face when you get home from school. And you've forgotten several times to tell me where you're going or if you'll be late. And you never sit down to eat your meals—you're always running through the house, to the phone, just to call

Tamara. As if you don't have enough time together at school! It's as if she's suddenly becoming your whole life. What about your other friends, Rachel and—"

"Mom . . . Rachel is your friend's daughter. I never liked her very much."

"Well, if you like Tamara so much, why don't you invite her over?"

"I have."

"Then why hasn't she come?"

"She's busy."

"Too busy to come over to her best friend's house?" Mom shook her head. "Have you really asked her?"

"Yes." I nodded.

"And she's said no?"

I nodded again.

"Leah, you're old enough to see there's something wrong."

"Tamara's a different sort of person, Mom. She's private—very private."

"What is it you like about Tamara? I'd like to hear."

"She knows a lot about life, and she knows how to be her own self, and we have a good time together."

"Doing what?"

"What is this? Do I have to report everything to you?"

"I want to meet her," Mom whispered. "And if she won't come on her own, I'll get hold of her mother and ask the entire family over for dinner."

"Mom! You can't force them to come. What are you trying to do, ruin things with my best friend?"

"That's the last thing I want to do. But what you've told me about Tamara concerns me." Mom paused. "And you're at an age when friends have a lot of influence. . . . I just want to meet her."

37

"You don't trust my judgment?"

"Leah, why are you trying to make me into the bad guy?"

"Why do you have to get involved—you won't even let me pick my own friends!"

"Humor me, Leah. I work with young people every day. I can't help but worry. You've got to choose friends carefully and—

"And what?" I yelled. "You tell me I'm spending too much time around Tamara and you say that I've changed—what about you? Look at all the time you spend with José! Look how you've changed—you're getting fat! But I don't try to pick out another man for you, even though I have much better taste!" Once I started yelling, I couldn't stop. "When you start choosing your friends carefully—then I'll start choosing my friends carefully. Follow your own advice. If you want to have a say in my life, then I should have a say in your life!"

"Leah, I'm your mother."

"And I'm your daughter. So what? Just because we're related doesn't mean you can run my life."

"This whole conversation is exactly what I'm talking about. You never used to talk to me this way. Does Tamara talk to her mother like this?"

"Her mother lets her lead her own life."

"Leah, what if I were spending part of every day with José and I never let you meet him—wouldn't you wonder why? Wouldn't you suspect something awful about him?"

"I began to suspect him after I met him."

"Your attitude convinces me it's time I meet Tamara."

"You're always convinced you're right, anyway, no matter what I say. So why do we even have these talks?"

I didn't wait to hear her answer. I ran to my room and

closed the door. And just to show her, I pulled the telephone into my bedroom and dialed Tamara's number. But
when I heard Tamara's voice, I hung up. How could I tell
Tamara about my fight with Mom, that Mom suspected her
even before she'd ever met her?

8

Tamara's always asking me questions about my father. Ever since I told her my dad's a professional skier and showed her a photograph of Dad and me, standing in front of his log cabin, Tamara's been obsessed. She always wants to know more about him.

"Do you ever fight?"

"Not really. I never really get mad at Dad. He's not the type."

"Then why don't you live with him?"

Living with Dad wouldn't be bad, but living with Lucy, Dad's girlfriend, would be the worst.

I told Tamara the story about the last time I visited Dad, when Lucy and I got into a big fight. I borrowed one of Dad's scarves without asking, because I never ask Dad for things; we just aren't like that. And he borrows stuff of mine, too, like pens and candy bars. It's just understood between us. But Lucy got mad.

"Isn't that the scarf I bought for your father?" she asked, referring to the one I had wrapped around my neck.

"Yeah, I guess," I said, brushing my hair.

"Yes, it is," Lucy repeated. Then, when she saw me starting to leave, she said, "I bought that for your father to match his sweater."

"It's beautiful," I said, and grabbed my mittens.

"It's not yours"—she paused—"to wear."

So I took off the scarf and threw it in her face. "Too bad Dad hates things that match!"

Later I purposely borrowed Dad's pajama tops and wore them like a nightie. I kept walking past Lucy until she finally noticed. "Does your father know you wear his things?"

I nodded. "In our family we share."

Later Dad came in and sat on my bed. "Lucy's jealous of you," he told me. It was hard to believe, since I'm Dad's daughter, but I knew it was true. Whenever I visit Dad, she stares at me, watching to see how I do things. And sometimes she copies, which is weird for a thirty-year-old woman. That's when Dad told me we'd have to include Lucy in more things, which is hard, because, to be completely honest, Lucy's a drag. She gets really nervous about almost everything.

On the last day of my visit Lucy hugged me and wrapped the scarf, the one she'd given Dad, around my neck. "I thought it looked better on you, anyway," she said. I saw her look at Dad, and when he smiled at her, I knew they had talked. It was weird because, after seeing them

41

look at each other that way, I felt like I had won something little, but lost something big.

"Well, who do you like best, Lucy or José?" Tamara asked after I told her about Lucy. "I mean, there has to be a lesser of two evils, right?"

"Well, Lucy's dumb and pretty. And José's smart and ugly. So it's hard to choose."

"Maybe if your parents see each other again, they'll get back together."

"No way."

And I told Tamara the whole story about how Mom and Dad met while she was taking ski lessons from him. Then I told Tamara that I had known we were leaving Colorado, even before Mom told me. Suzy, my cousin, was visiting, and she told me Dad liked another woman better than Mom. I was only nine at the time, but I remember we were going up the chair lift on Downer's Peak, which is the longest ride up the mountain. It never occurred to me that what Suzy was saying might be true.

"It's just one of his privates," I told Suzy. Dad makes most of his money teaching private lessons to rich people, mostly women, and lots of times he has to teach at night on one of the slopes with lights.

I didn't talk to Suzy the rest of the way up the mountain.

"Don't be mad, please," she begged. "I just didn't want you to feel stupid when they tell you."

Each time Suzy fell going down the mountain, I felt better.

A couple of days later Mom told me that she and I were moving to Milwaukee, where Grandma lived in a nursing home. "We'll alternate holidays, and you'll spend half the summer with Daddy. How does that sound?" Mom was braiding my hair when she told me, and the braids were too tight because she wasn't paying any attention to what she was doing.

"Loosen it, Mom." I jerked away and felt the braid fall apart. "Why can't we stay here?" I demanded.

"Someday you'll understand," Mom said.

More than anything I hate when parents say, "Someday you'll understand."

"I do understand," I yelled at her. "Daddy's got someone he likes better. Why do you have to treat me like a two-year-old? I know all about it!" I felt terrible watching Mom's face soften, her chin quiver. "Mom, don't," I said, "please don't cry." After that Mom always used Dad's name, Peter, instead of calling him Daddy like before.

"That's the thing about Mom," I told Tamara, "it's not worth crying around her because she starts crying too. Or at least she used to, before she met José."

"That's how women are," Tamara said. "Between boyfriends Bette's unbearable too. She cries all the time."

"So, when are you going to visit your dad?" she repeated. "Could I go with you?"

Then I told her about last night's phone call. Dad is always unreliable, especially about the dates of my visits. So when I heard his voice on the phone, I figured he was going to tell me to come on a different day.

"Honey, I hate to do this, but I've got a problem with this Christmas. I think maybe it's better if we postpone your visit."

At first I thought he meant postpone it by a day or two, like usual, but then there was this long pause, and I knew he meant postpone it past the whole vacation. "But, Dad—"

"Honey, it's not my fault. I'm just so short this season.

43

I've had to line up private lessons every night, just to make ends meet. That leaves us almost no time."

Dad had never canceled one of my trips before.

"Dad, I can take care of myself." One thing about talking to Dad is that I never say exactly what I think. Mostly because by the time I realize what I'm feeling, Dad's already hung up. I wanted to tell him that I really needed to see him this time—I needed to get away from Mom and José.

"Leah, don't be mad. I'm hoping to make it to Chicago the weekend of your grandma's birthday in January, okay? You can take the train down, we'll spend a weekend together then."

"Can I bring a friend?"

"We'll talk about it."

That was it. Dad said good-bye and hung up. And I just sat there thinking of all the things I should have said.

After Dad called, Mom tapped at my door. "Can I come in?"

I moved over to the side so Mom could sit with her legs up on my bed.

"What'd Peter say about your visit?"

"He said he's got to cancel my visit."

"I see." Mom nodded. "And is that okay with you?"

"I guess so," I lied. "It's just that I told everyone I would be going to Colorado for Christmas." Mom handed me a Kleenex because I'd started to cry and I couldn't breathe very well. "And Dad's always the same. Everything's got to revolve around his schedule."

Mom hugged me. "Leah, sometimes Peter reacts to me through you, probably without realizing it."

"That's your point of view."

Mom nodded. "Yes, it is my point of view." She smiled.

44

"I think Peter's very upset because José is spending so much time with me. Peter has told me as much."

"When did you call Daddy?"

"I called to see if you could spend an extra week with him this Christmas." Mom paused. "José and I were hoping to go to Mexico."

"Why didn't you tell me?"

Mom smiled, and then it registered—I wasn't invited to Mexico! Mom was planning a vacation without me. And she'd never even mentioned it! "What about the vacation you promised me?"

"I said as soon as I finished my M.A. we'd go to Yellowstone."

"God, Mom, anyplace but Yellowstone. Why can't we go to Mexico?"

"Why not Yellowstone?" she asked.

"It's a place for families."

Her voice sank. "Aren't we a family?"

"Mom, national parks are for parents with three kids packed into station wagons with their windows closed while the kids point at bears eating peanut-butter sandwiches out of trash cans."

"When were you there?"

"Let's skip the vacation and go shopping," I told her.

"I worry about your generation," she said, shaking her head. "No soul, no values." Mom paused. "Anyway, your dad's worried about José's influence on you."

"He should be worried!"

"Peter's already judged him." I could hear the anger in her voice. "He wanted to know if José spoke English and if he had a job. He even asked if José was legal."

"Wait till Dad sees how he dresses and combs his hair. Then he'll really freak."

45

"That's why it's really important for you to tell Peter how nice José is, and that you like him. So Peter won't worry."

"What did Dad say when you asked him if I could stay longer?"

"He said he'd think about it and talk to Lucy."

"So Lucy must have said no. God, I hate her!"

Mom hugged me. "Give it time, and tell Peter how you feel. Did you tell him tonight that you were hurt?"

I shook my head.

"Why not? Why don't you tell him?"

I shrugged. "Do you ever miss Daddy?"

Mom sat up. "Sometimes. There aren't many free spirits left in this world. Peter's probably one of the last."

"I am too," I said.

Mom smiled and shook her head. "It's harder for women to be free spirits," she said. "I know, I tried."

"Just wait," I told her. "I'm going to live in a cabin on a mountain and teach skiing."

Later, when I was almost asleep, Mom came in and sat on my bed. As she looked out the window where the street-lights were filtering through the bamboo blind, Mom started massaging my back. "I never thought we'd stay in Colorado, not in Steamboat anyway. It's a place where people vacation, not a place where people live. And I never thought of making a career out of skiing. That was what Peter wanted, not me. Then after you were born, I realized Peter didn't plan on changing. He never intended to leave, but I wanted to go back to school. It never felt real to me there. Do you know what I'm saying?"

"But why'd you marry Dad if you didn't want the same things?"

"No two people want exactly the same things out of life.

46

But I was young then. It was hard for me to be different from the people I loved—to want different things from them. I thought loving them meant wanting exactly the same life as they led."

"You and José don't want the same things?"

"With José it's okay for me to feel different about situations and to want different kinds of experiences. He accepts that. I guess what I'm trying to tell you is that it's hard to love someone and to be yourself, but it's important. Remember that, Leah. I don't want you to repeat my mistakes."

"God, Mom, I'm not your clone."

Mom smiled and kissed me on the cheek. Then, just when I was starting to feel close to Mom again, she whispered. "So, when do I get to meet Tamara?"

"Good night, Mom."

"So, I guess, if Dad comes," I told Tamara, "I'll see him in January."

"Can I meet him?"

"Maybe. If he lets me bring a guest."

"He sounds fabulous. What if we just showed up in Colorado sometime and surprised him?"

"Lucy's not the type that likes surprises."

"But your Dad likes to have fun, right?"

I grinned. "Mom calls him the last of the free spirits. She says men can be free spirits but not women."

Tamara rolled her eyes and scowled. "Women can be as free as men. I do exactly as I please, when I please."

"In a lot of ways you're like my father, you know how to have a good time."

47

Tamara looked at me with a strange expression. "That's why mothers don't like me, and I don't like mothers."

Then she grinned. "But fathers are another matter. I think I'd get along with your dad." She blushed as she spoke, and I realized then she had a crush on my father, even though she'd never met him.

"Tamara, he's my father!"

"So? The average age difference between Bette and most of her husbands is about thirty years . . . your Dad's thirty-nine and I'm almost fifteen—that's only twenty-four years between us!

9

Tamara asked me to go to this benefit called a Psychic Tea on Saturday. "It's a tax write-off for Bette," she confided.

I had never heard of anything like that, but Tamara explained that there would be handwriting experts, massage therapists, healers, and astrologists. Mrs. Luchio calls them spiritual artists.

"That's Mom's disguise," Tamara stated. "She pretends to be a really spiritual human being—not the subhuman she really is."

"What does she do there?" I asked.

"She runs it . . . that's how she uses her money. She sponsors these things."

"Who comes to them?"

"Lots of people. You don't have to believe in this sort of thing to come." Tamara leaned close. "I even stuffed a brochure down the slits of Caesar's locker, and I wrote a note on the back, *Your future will be revealed.*"

"You're kidding!"

"No, I'm not, and it's the truth," Tamara said, breaking into a grin. "I'm his future."

Anyway, Mrs. Luchio knew this really famous astrologist, Mari Setzun, who said she'd tell us about our signs, and Tamara said her predictions are always right. Normally people have to pay lots of money to see her, but since she's a friend of Mrs. Luchio, we would get to go free. Only, Tamara would have to call her in advance and give her the exact times and places we were born.

"You were born sometime in the afternoon," Mom told me when I asked her.

"Mom, it has to be exact."

Mom was doing her students' psychological evaluations, which always puts her in a bad mood. "Most of these kids don't have half a chance. . . ." she said, shaking her head. Then she stared at me. "Leah, stuff like astrology is for desperate people. You can read your life into anything those people say. It's a racket!"

Just because Mom decided to be a social worker, she expects everyone to suffer with her, take on the burdens of the world.

I didn't want to fight with Mom about it, so I just looked through her desk and found my birth certificate and some other forms from the hospital that listed my height and weight. I was born at seven thirty-eight A.M. on September twenty-fifth.

50

A week later, when I told Mom I was going to the Psychic Tea with Mrs. Luchio and Tamara, and that I'd be gone all day, Mom got upset. "I thought I told you I wanted you to skip that event."

"You didn't say that. You said you were too busy to find my birth information."

"Yes, and the reason I was too busy is because I didn't want you to go . . . there are a lot of weirdos and crooks at that sort of function."

"Mom, I'll be with Tamara and her mother—don't worry."

Mom hesitated. "On one condition. If I say yes, you have to promise me you'll ask Tamara to come join us for Thanksgiving. José will be here with some of his family, and I'd like you to invite your friend. If Tamara wants to, she can bring her brother and mother. How's that sound? We haven't had a real party around here for at least a year."

"Not another Thanksgiving party!" I groaned.

"This year will be different—lots of food, lots of people, and lots of fun."

"You sound like a commercial for Pepperidge Farm stuffing." Every year, around Thanksgiving, Mom invites all the people she knows who have no place else to go. And, in my opinion, the reason they have no place to go is because they are depressing people. They have nothing in common with each other, so the entire meal is spent in silence. Mom and me struggling to keep the conversation going.

"Couldn't the two of us go out?"

"I've already invited José's family, and I want you to invite Tamara."

"Mom, I'm sure they already have plans."

"Ask them. If you don't ask them, then I will. I'm serious, Leah. You're spending every weekend with Tamara

51

and her family, and I want to meet them. It's final. If you don't ask them today, then I'm going to get hold of Mrs. Luchio myself. Even if I have to send a written invitation."

I got on my coat and turned to leave. "Okay, okay," I assured her, but Tamara had already made it clear, she had no intention of meeting Mom.

The Psychic Tea was really different from what I'd expected. When we arrived at the Marriott Hotel where the tea was taking place, the banquet room had white table-cloths and bouquets of flowers at each booth. Mrs. Luchio looked very elegant. She wore a navy suit with high heels, and her hair was woven in an intricate bun on top of her head.

Mrs. Luchio knew everyone and introduced us to her friends and, as usual, Tamara refused to call the adults by their last names. That's one of the reasons I was afraid to introduce her to Mom. If Tamara called Mom "Jessica," Mom would lose her cool. She'd tell Tamara right off not to be so disrespectful.

Mari, the astrologist, had her booth set up in a private room because she was the most famous person there. We went in and sat in leather chairs while she looked at our charts—that's what she called them. Tamara had called and told her our birth times earlier in the week, so she was all prepared. She had pages with circles and lines drawn on them, and she told us about our houses, the rising and setting signs and planets. She did Tamara's chart first and spoke in an even tone. "Your planets are moving through a very stable period, without much change."

Tamara looked disappointed. "Yeah?"

"You're a very independent person. You like to work alone. You need autonomy, which probably means you have a difficult time in school—am I correct?"

Tamara nodded.

"And there's a lot of Taurus in your sign—very strong willed, right?"

Tamara laughed and nodded again.

"You're very creative and ambitious," Mari continued. "But you're not in a prolific period, meaning your creativity has yet to reach its full potential. Your planets are stabilizing, so you may be in for a rest—which isn't bad, we all need times like that." Mari smiled.

Tamara looked angry. "Any sign of romance?"

Mari lifted her eyebrows. "I can't say for sure." Then she made some suggestions for the coming year and handed the chart to Tamara.

"That's it? That's all you can tell me?" Tamara asked angrily.

"You get to keep the chart for future reference." Mari smiled.

Tamara lifted the chart and tore it into tiny pieces, right in front of Mari.

"Your turn," Mari said calmly, nodding toward me. She paused and looked at my chart. "Your planet is going through several major changes. Extreme shifts, perhaps with your family or friends." She looked up and stared at me. "There may be some loss, but whenever there's loss, there's also gain."

I nodded.

"I think there will be someone special in your life, perhaps an older man, someone who will become very instrumental in your life." I got really excited hearing Mari say that, and I looked at Tamara, but she just rolled her eyes and pouted. I didn't completely believe Mari's predictions, not entirely, but I liked to think about them.

I guess I was thinking out loud because later, when we

53

were watching the handwriting experts, Tamara said we should talk about something else. "How do you even know if Mari's right?" Tamara asked, shrugging and walking away from me. "I don't believe a word she said—she's as crazy as Bette!"

One thing about Tamara, if she's in a bad mood, she ruins everyone else's mood too. And the fact that Caesar hadn't shown up for the Psychic Tea only made Tamara angrier about Mari's predictions.

Tamara insisted we leave the Psychic Tea early and get a hamburger at the Oriental Drugstore on the way home. "That's where he and his friends hang out," she whispered.

"How do you know?"

"I know."

I waited until the waitress brought our malts, then I asked her. "Tamara"—I hesitated—"Mom really wants to meet you, and she wants to know if you could come for Thanksgiving. . . . José will be there with some other people." Even before I had finished my statement, I saw her eyes look away and I already knew what she'd say.

"Can't. Leonard's coming for dinner that day. Mom's going to finish him off if she can . . . you know, lots of buttered dressing and rolls with lathered butter and turkey with butter gravy. It's Mom's favorite holiday because she can do what she does best without arousing any suspicions. You should see all the whipped cream she puts on the pumpkin pie. She might as well just inject it directly into his arteries."

"But couldn't you come for just a little while, long enough for Mom to meet you? You could even bring Bette and Leonard and Jake."

"Oh, great. Introduce my mother to your mother so they can complain about us for hours. Leonard and José can sit in a corner and discuss sports. Sounds like a great holiday."

I was getting desperate. "Look, Mom says if you're my best friend, which you are, then she wants to get to know you too. So if you don't say yes, she might even call your mom herself."

Tamara looked at me with an expression that I'd never seen before. She seemed nervous, "Why is your mom being so pushy?"

"She's not. She just likes to know my friends."

"Why?"

I couldn't tell Tamara the truth . . . that Mom thought Tamara sounded disturbed. "It's just the way Mom is. Look, if you come, you can talk to José about California."

"True." Tamara looked off in the distance, as if she had to consider her options.

"I'll think about it and talk it over with Bette."

We sat in silence until our food arrived, and just as I'd begun to enjoy my chocolate malt, I saw Tamara's eyes grow wide. She was looking behind me.

"God, you'll never guess who walked in here. He's buying a magazine."

I turned and saw Caesar and his friend at the magazine rack.

"Don't look," Tamara whispered. "God, they'll know we're talking about them. We've got to do something!" Tamara said, pushing her plate away. "Don't let them see us porking out."

Suddenly Caesar's friend, Nathan, started walking toward the lunch counter where we were sitting.

"Oh, God, why did we order malts and hamburgers, they'll think we're pigs." Tamara whispered, but then, smil-

55

ing as if she'd never been happier, she turned to Caesar and said, "Hi." Like she'd been expecting him. He said hi, too, as they took a place two seats down from us.

My stomach was in knots. Tamara looked at me and started talking loudly, but I couldn't concentrate on what she was saying, something about a concert coming to town.

Then, when the two ladies sitting next to us stood up, she looked at Caesar and smiled again, nodding at the vacant seats. "Why don't you guys move over and sit here?" Just like she'd been studying the line all her life. That's what I found so incredible about Tamara—she was smooth.

They moved over two seats. "Aren't you going to eat that?" Caesar asked, pointing to the plate Tamara had pushed away.

"No, it's way too much food. Do you want it?"

Tamara pushed both our plates over in their direction.

Caesar looked at me for a few seconds, then nodded. "I know where I've seen you. You live near Capitol Drive, right? I used to bag groceries at the store there. You and your mom came in all the time."

I didn't remember him, but I nodded.

"That was a year ago. I was filling in for my older brother."

"Yeah." I smiled. "We still live there." It felt great, he'd actually recognized me! Tamara had to be impressed!

But Tamara suddenly looked at her watch, "Oh, God, we've got to get going. Remember?"

I looked at her. Remember what?

"They're picking us up at eight."

I hesitated, watching her face turn red. "Oh, yeah."

"The concert begins at nine." Her voice was insistent.

"Right."

"See you around, then." Tamara grabbed her purse and

I followed her, whispering good-bye without looking the boys in the eyes.

Outside, Tamara was silent.

"Why did we leave? Why did you make up that story?"

Tamara stared at the passing cars and remained silent.

"What's the matter?" I whispered. "Aren't you glad we talked to them?"

"If you aren't careful," Tamara stated defiantly, "you'll turn out to be worse than Bette!"

"What'd I do wrong?" I asked.

"You flirted with Caesar."

"We talked only because he recognized me. He sat next to you, though!"

"I was closest," she said. "He barely looked at me."

"Tamara, he would have talked to you, but we left. I know he likes you."

"Really? Why?" She suddenly looked hopeful.

"Just the way he sat, you know, sort of leaning in your direction."

Tamara grinned. "God, he's so beautiful. Those muscles!"

"Why did we have to leave, then?"

Tamara rolled her eyes. "We don't want them to think we're going to wait around forever."

"But we barely talked to them."

"Guys like them don't talk much. That's what I like about them."

"Why do you like that?"

"Mystery," Tamara stated, but her smile faded quickly.

"What's wrong?"

"We didn't give them our names."

"There wasn't time."

"Well, that's their problem, isn't it." Tamara started walking toward the park.

"Yeah," I whispered doubtfully, "their problem!"

When I got home, Mom immediately demanded, "Did you ask her?"

I nodded.

"And?"

"And she said she'd talk to Bette."

"Who's Bette?"

"Her mother."

"Since when do you call your friends' parents by their first names?"

"I don't, Tamara does."

I looked at Mom—sometimes when she was dressed for bed, I got a kind of ache. Mom looks really pretty when she's dressed up, but before bed, her hair loses its curl, and her skin's always washed shiny. She pads around the house with her furry slippers, the ones I hate because the pink fur got wet once, and ever since, it's matted and clumped-looking. Before bed there's something about Mom, maybe the smell of soap and powder, that makes her seem old. Whenever I see her like that, I realize that someday she might not be there, and I feel an ache gnawing inside me.

"What are you looking at?" she asked. She looked down at her front. "I'm dieting, as of today. José and I are both going to lose weight."

"That's not why I was looking at you."

"You said the other day that I'm fat."

Suddenly I went over and hugged Mom.

"Are you okay?" she asked.

"Mmm-hmmm." I turned to leave. Inside, though, I was thinking about Thanksgiving. I felt like Tamara and Mom weren't the same type of person. And that scared me, because what would I do then?

58

10

Mom invited Grandma Lucas, Dad's mom, to spend Thanksgiving with us. She lives in a huge house outside Chicago with a maid named Rita. But Grandma said she couldn't come visit over the holiday, and Mom thinks it's because of José, because he's Mexican.

All week Mom and José have been preparing stuff for the Thanksgiving party—pumpkin pies, mincemeat pies, fresh loaves of French bread, cranberry relish, wild rice with raisins and nuts, and lots more.

Having José in the house every day this week, while he and Mom were cooking, was a pain. Before Mom started dating José, I felt like all the rooms in the apartment were mine. But lately, wherever José is, whatever space he takes up, I have to be polite about it.

At Dad's place I can just tell him I want to be alone, and he'll go into the other room. Sometimes I'll just say, "I got this room first," which means I get to choose the TV program or I get the whole couch to myself. Dad always gets the message. But with José I have to be more polite or he and Mom take it wrong. "Which program do you want to see?" I ask, and he says, "Whatever you're watching." But I know he's just waiting for my program to end so he can watch football. Sometimes I just want to read on the couch, and he comes in and starts reading the newspaper in the rocking chair. Then I can't concentrate anymore. I hear him breathe and clear his throat, and it's like I'm the visitor.

Even though I liked having the apartment smell so good —all the breads and pies baking—it made me nervous to see Mom and José having so much fun in the kitchen. Once I heard Mom laughing really hard, and I went in to see what was going on. Mom pointed to José dancing on the floor, using a broom for his partner.

"He's doing the Santiago shuffle." She giggled.

José bowed. "Want a lesson, Leah?"

I just shook my head. Tamara told me to think of it as a challenge to see how little I could say to him and still be polite. It was hard seeing them have so much fun, when I didn't have anyone special in my own life. I grabbed a handful of cookies and headed for my room. Just when I was settling into my homework, I heard a knock, and Mom came in smiling. "We're counting plates and silverware for Thursday. Do you think Tamara's going to bring her whole family?"

"I don't know," I said.

Mom giggled. "After all, it's not everyday you can eat

60

Thanksgiving dinner with a woman who murders with food!"

"Mom, Tamara won't be coming for very long—she's just going to drop in."

Mom's face lost its smile. "Leah, you did ask her, right? Promise?"

I nodded.

"Okay, then, we'll just make sure we have plenty for whoever shows up."

All Wednesday I kept asking Tamara about her plans for the next four days. She mentioned she was going to go to the Mall on Saturday and asked if I'd like to go with her.

"Sure," I replied, wondering if I'd have to beg her to come to Mom's party the next day.

"See you at the bus stop, then, Saturday, around noon," Tamara said, running for her bus. I knew then she had no intention of coming over for Thanksgiving dinner.

When I got home Mom was waiting for me, her expression furious. "Leah, you lied."

"About what?" I asked, totally surprised.

"You didn't ask Tamara. I called the school today and got Mrs. Luchio's number and called her myself, just to let her know we'd love to have the whole family, and she told me Tamara hadn't mentioned the invitation. She also said she and Tamara would love to come!"

Mom turned her back to me. "What's so terrible about me, José, or this apartment that you can't bring your friends home? We aren't monsters! José is wonderful with young people—the students love him!"

Sure! He's not in love with their mother, I thought.

61

Mom turned and her eyes softened, "Leah, tell me why. . . ."

But there was no way to explain without admitting that Tamara was the real liar, and that would finish it for Tamara. They'd never get along.

"Mrs. Luchio told me how glad she is that Tamara has you for a friend. She certainly didn't sound like the kind of woman who'd kill off husbands."

"She can wrap anyone around her finger," I said. "Don't let appearances fool you."

"I'm not worried about appearances, I'm worried about you." Mom stared at me. "Mrs. Luchio was delighted by our invitation. She and Tamara were going to have to spend Thanksgiving by themselves because Jake is visiting a friend and Bette's boyfriend, Leonard, is going to New York to visit his mother."

So Tamara had lied to me about Leonard spending Thanksgiving with them too.

Mom smiled, "I'm a little nervous . . . with José's family coming. Be on your best behavior, okay?"

How could I be on my best behavior with Tamara here —Tamara would never forgive me if I were nice to José's family.

"I asked Bette to bring Tamara a little early, so we'd have a few minutes to talk before everyone else arrives. That way the Luchios won't feel outnumbered."

"Great, Mom, great." Anything else you want to tell me about my best friend?

11

When I opened the door Thanksgiving morning to bring in the newspaper, Grandma was driving up to the house. I yelled in to Mom, who was making coffee, and she let out a loud groan. Grandma's the sort of person who comes to a party out of obligation—not because she wanted to meet Mom's friends. And if she didn't come, she'd feel guilty for the next year. You see, Grandma gets depressed about small things, like my posture. She constantly tells me to keep my shoulders back or I'll get a hump when I turn her age.

"It can ruin your looks. Someone tall like you should never allow that to happen."

She tells me my clothes should be ironed, and if Mom

63

won't do it, then they should be done professionally. "If it's a matter of money . . ." Then she'll pull out her purse.

But Mom has a rule about not accepting money from Grandma Lucas unless it's a Christmas present. Mom hugged Grandma as she approached the front door. "What time did you get up this morning, Muriel?"

"Four-thirty, but I'm up anyway at that hour, and I wanted to beat the traffic. I knew there would be something I could do to help. Who hasn't had breakfast?" Grandma asked as she looked at me. "What do I always tell you. . . . The rest of your meals are worthless if you don't eat when you get up—that's when you need your energy."

I can only stand Grandma for small amounts of time. It's sort of like being in the army—that's what Dad says it was like for him when he was growing up. He still calls Grandma Sergeant. Mom says that Grandma's rules are what made Dad the way he is—he hates schedules. He won't stick to any routine. And he'll do things for you, but only as long as you never ask him to do them.

After breakfast we all started in on our duties. Grandma helped me with the dusting and vacuuming until midmorning, when the doorbell rang. As I opened the door, I almost didn't recognize José.

"Hey, Leah." He walked into the living room. "Thought I'd come help with the turkey."

"Mom's in the kitchen"—I paused—"with Grandma, my dad's mom." I was amazed to see José so dressed up—blue suit, white shirt, striped tie. Of course, everything he wore was tight, his shirt bulged over his belt and his neck squeezed out of his collar. But for the first time he did look all right. His hair was combed back and his eyes matched his suit.

Then I noticed his feet—he was wearing rubbers. He'd

worn them to protect his good shoes from getting wet, just like I used to do in grammar school. There was something about those rubbers at the bottom of his body that made me realize I didn't know him at all. I suddenly felt guilty, not because of his rubbers exactly, but because I felt he was trying so hard to make a good impression, and I hadn't tried at all.

Mom and Grandma both appeared in the hallway. "José, my mother-in-law surprised us this morning, isn't that great?" Mom laughed nervously. "Muriel, this is José; José, this is Leah's grandmother, Muriel."

They shook hands, and Grandma looked him over. "How do you do."

José nodded. "It's great you could come over. My whole family will be here."

Grandma glanced at Mom.

"We've invited about twenty people. We're even going to finally get to meet Leah's new friend."

"Well, I'm not sure if I can stay through the whole thing. . . ."

Mom took Grandma's coat. "Oh, Muriel, you're here, so you might as well enjoy it."

Grandma sighed and stared at José. "Can your apartment hold his whole family?" She smiled. "I'm sure there are lots of them."

Mom's face reddened.

José blushed, but his glance at Mom told her to let him handle it. "There will be ten of us," José stated. "My family will be especially delighted to meet you."

I went into the bedroom and started tidying up. So far the day could only improve.

*　　*　　*

José's mother had wanted to bring some of the meal, and for some reason I'd expected hot, spicy stuff. But when Mrs. Santiago arrived, she brought two hams with pineapple sauce and loaves of pumpkin and cranberry bread. Plus, she had brought flowers in a beautiful white vase.

"These are for you," she whispered to Mom. "A gift."

I watched Grandma circulate and look over José's family—his brother and his wife, their baby, José's mother, her two sisters, and their husbands. No one close to my age, I realized with relief.

I had expected José's family to be shy, but they weren't like that. Uncle Ramón kept filling everyone's glass with wine, including mine, until I started to feel light and dizzy. That's when Mom told me to pass the hors d'oeuvres and get something in my stomach.

I kept wondering why Tamara and Bette hadn't arrived —the party had been going on for at least an hour, and in a few minutes the dinner would be served.

I watched José's family—he was the only fat one. The rest were small and thin and dark. His mother was beautiful, with dark, smooth skin and big eyes, and her hair, which had turned white, was pulled back in a bun. José's sister was heavier than her mother, but pretty, too, and his brother, although stocky like José, had huge muscles. If Tamara met him, she'd go crazy.

One of the twin aunts came over and sat next to me. "You're Leah. I've heard so much about you and your mother."

I nodded. She seemed to lean back, focusing her eyes on my entire face, as if to see whether I was listening.

"I understand your mother has raised you by herself."

"I visit my father in the summers."

66

She smiled a thin smile. "Oh, I see. Your parents were divorced a long time ago?"

"Yes."

"Then they're not Catholic."

"No. Dad's Episcopalian, and Mom's Methodist."

"It must be terribly hard on your mother, having to work, and raising you by herself. What does she do if you get sick—does she stay home from work?"

"Only when I was little. Now she goes to work and calls me every hour to see if I'm okay."

The little aunt's eyes grew wide. "I suppose she has no choice."

I nodded slightly.

"We're Catholic, you see."

"Yeah, José told me about it."

She smiled. "Catholics don't believe in divorce."

I thought of the Luchios, they were Catholic. That's when I burst out laughing, right in the middle of the room. The aunt thought I was being rude and whispered something to Mrs. Santiago, who handed me a plate of turkey with dressing, then guided me over to a seat in the corner of the dining room.

Mom asked if I was all right, and when I nodded, she whispered, "You're getting the third degree too?"

I didn't know exactly what she meant, but I could tell Mom was having too much to drink. Her eyes were lit up, her cheeks flushed.

"Where are the Luchios? Did they call?" Mom asked, glancing toward the clock on the mantel.

"I don't know, you never know with Tamara."

"Why don't you call them and see if they can hurry. We're about to tell everyone to serve themselves."

I looked around and realized I was the only one eating.

67

I considered calling Tamara but decided against it. Mom didn't understand—Tamara was the kind of person who hated family gatherings like this. For one thing, there weren't any single guys, so she'd be bored.

As I sat there eating, I heard a knock on the back door, and when I opened it, this guy came in carrying a crate of wine. He nodded toward the counter, indicating I should move the plates, so he could set down his crate.

"Thanks, this weighs a ton."

He was out of breath, sweat dripping down the side of his face. "José!" He called. "Sorry, but none of the stores nearby were open. I had to go all the way to the Mall."

I thought he was the delivery boy until José hugged him. "Leah, this is my notorious nephew, Miguel." José turned and faced me. "This is Jessica's daughter, Leah."

"Sorry . . . I'm late." He smiled at José, then turned and stared at me, his big eyes unflinching, until I wanted to disappear right into the carpet. "I'm starved too. Save me a place."

I watched as Miguel set a couple of bottles on the bar and helped himself to a plate of food. He didn't seem the least bit self-conscious about piling his plate with food and helping himself to wine in someone else's home. I felt relaxed from the wine, but still, I didn't know what I'd say when he sat down next to me. I had never known boys like Miguel. I mean, I knew Mexican guys, but at my school in Shorewood, the Mexican kids are like everyone else. They're all preppy. But Miguel dressed different, sort of. Not like José, who normally dressed in old clothes. Miguel dressed up. His shirt was bright blue, tight, and unbottoned halfway down, like he wanted to show off his chest and muscles. And his pants were blue jeans, but more of a designer style that guys at my school would never wear. Then he had a leather jacket, which he immediately took off. But what I noticed most were his shoes. I guess they were dress shoes, but even so, none of the guys I knew would be caught dead in shoes like that—black leather with inch-high heels and pointy toes, plus they were way too shiny. Then, where his shirt was unbuttoned, was this huge cross on a chain. How could someone who dresses like him wear a gold cross, I wondered. He didn't look religious!

When he passed a glass of wine in my direction, my voice came out way too high. "Thanks."

"No problem." He flashed a big smile. We ate for a few seconds before either of us broke the silence. It seemed like even while Miguel was eating, some part of his body was always moving—his foot, or his leg, or his shoulders, kept shifting positions. At first I thought he was nervous, or maybe he just couldn't get comfortable.

When he finished what was on his plate, he kind of shifted his position so he was facing me, leaning back against the wall, with his shoulders arched back. "José told me you go to Shorewood," he stated.

"I'm a freshman," I said, avoiding his eyes.

"You mean freshwoman!" He laughed under his breath. "I've been to your school before." But the tone of his laughter wasn't clear to me. Was he making fun of me? Shorewood has the reputation of being the snobbiest school in the city: did he think I was that way?

"I was in a recital there last year," he added. "Your teachers aren't bad."

I knew he meant they were good, really good. Everyone knew Shorewood's one of the best high schools.

"Aren't you going to ask what instrument I play? Aren't you overwhelmed by curiosity?" Again his voice

69

shifted, this time flirting and teasing at the same time. His smile widened, and his eyes narrowed just the slightest bit. Even when I wasn't looking directly at him, I could feel his eyes, a sort of heat, climbing my body.

"What kind?" My voice wavered. He and I both knew he was making me nervous—it was his dark eyes and long lashes. I felt his eyes could see right through me. And maybe it was the way he sat with his shoulders back and his body—all that muscle—right there practically touching me. It was embarrassing to even look up. And when I forced myself to, I kept seeing his cross, and behind his cross, his dark smooth chest. Then I'd force myself to look away because I didn't want him to see me staring.

"I played guitar at the recital," he said. "But now I'm learning the sax. Do you like jazz?"

I shrugged. "I don't know much about it."

He started drumming his thighs, humming a song. "Ever hear of it?" he asked, suddenly stopping.

I shook my head.

"Really? You've never heard that song?"

"No," I stated. "Is it on the radio a lot?"

Miguel laughed out loud. "I wrote it myself."

I stared at him. Inside I felt angry. Was he trying to make me feel like a fool?

"Hey, I'm just teasing, you know. I mean, I really did write it, but it's not on the radio. Not yet, anyway."

I drank some of my wine and looked at the people around the room. Where was Tamara when I needed her?

"One day I'll come over and give you a concert," Miguel suggested. "José keeps telling me to come over to your house and play for your mom so she'll see that someone in our family has talent." He grinned. "No, actually, he wants

70

to hear my latest tunes, so maybe now that I've met you, there's more incentive to come play for them!"

I couldn't stop the heat from climbing to my face, flooding my skin. I had never had a guy flirt with me so openly like that.

"What do you like to do?" he asked.

I looked at his smile—like to do?

"Do you go dancing? Do sports?" He nodded as he spoke, and suddenly I realized he was trying to help me talk.

"I baby-sit a lot."

"Yeah?" he said, like it was some big deal. "I work too. Off the record, that is. I fill in for a friend of mine who's got a job at Century Hall. He's been sick off and on for about six months, so I sweep the floors and wash dishes, mostly on weekends. Then he gives me the money from his paycheck. I get to listen to a lot of the bands from the kitchen, and the manager promised when I turn sixteen, I'll get my own job there."

My mind was working in slow motion. I tried to talk, but my mouth felt like elastic, as if I couldn't make the words bend the way I wanted them to. Partly it was due to the wine, but even more than that, it was because I sort of liked Miguel, and I didn't want to say anything stupid.

"Where do you go to school?" I forced myself to ask.

"Rufus King."

"You like it?"

"Sure," Miguel said, leaning back again. "My music classes, at least."

"So how old are you?"

"Sixteen next month." He paused. "I'm a sophomore." Then he shifted his position and added, "What I hate most about school is taking the bus back and forth, you know? We live on the South Side, so it's a long commute."

"Can't you carpool?"

Miguel laughed and shook his head. "Oh, sure, like my convertible Mercedes is in the garage, but only temporarily."

Why did he have to make a joke out of everything?

Then with a thick Spanish accent, he added, "I'm Mexican, you know? They bus the kids in my neighborhood to different schools!" He paused and smiled. "Not like the kids in the suburbs."

I guess the wine must have really hit me because, for once, I felt natural, and I was saying whatever came into my head. "You mean there's a lot of prejudice in Milwaukee, right?"

Miguel's eyebrows lifted as his smile widened. "Of course."

"Do you get angry about it?"

"Sometimes." Then he leaned toward me. "But not always." He was leaning so close, I could smell his shampoo, a minty smell. And when I looked up, his whole face was next to mine. "What angers me most is when people pretend not to notice my name, like if they call me Michael or Mikey, or if they're too nice, you know? Like if they automatically start talking about how great Mexican food is . . . stuff like that."

Just then Mrs. Santiago came up and passed a platter of almond cookies. "My special cookies." She smiled. "I see you two have met. He's a good boy," she said. "Miguel's all right."

She leaned over and kissed Miguel on the cheek, and he smiled at her. He didn't seem at all embarrassed to be kissing his grandmother in front of me.

Mrs. Santiago turned to me. "A friend of yours just arrived. Bette Luchio. José's with her."

I stood up and glanced around the room for Mom, but before I could spot her, I saw José leading Mrs. Luchio toward me.

12

Leah, have you seen Tamara?" Mrs. Luchio asked quickly. "I was hoping she'd be here already."

"No, she hasn't come yet."

Mom came over and I introduced her to Mrs. Luchio, who apologized for not having arrived earlier. "Tamara left this morning with her purse, and she hasn't been home all day. It's not like her."

Then she didn't know her daughter very well, I thought to myself.

"Leah, will you get Mrs. Luchio some dinner?"

"Oh, no." Mrs. Luchio put her hand up in the air. "Not this late. You've all finished."

Mom handed Mrs. Luchio a glass of wine. "We've finished with firsts, and we're about to get started on seconds."

I got Mrs. Luchio some food, then took a seat on one side of her while Mom sat on the other.

"How long have you lived on the East Side?" Mom asked, referring to the area where we lived along Lake Michigan.

"We've been here a year and a half. We came from Denver, where Tamara was raised."

"I understand you lost your first husband. . . . I'm sorry."

Mrs. Luchio raised her eyes and glanced at Mom as if she didn't quite understand.

"Tamara told Leah all about him," Mom added.

Mom glanced at me nervously, then turned again to Mrs. Luchio and asked, "And you've remarried since?"

"No." Bette blushed as she spoke. Then, almost defensively, she added, "Though I've had my chances." It was clear she was growing uncomfortable with Mom's questions. "These things take time. It's been especially hard on Tamara. Except for Saul, she's never liked the men I've dated, especially Leonard. She's at that age when she's jealous of the men in my life."

Who was lying, I wondered—Tamara or her mother? I walked to the table to get some dessert and saw Bette glance at me as she whispered, "Does Leah like José?"

"I think so," Mom said, smiling at me. "They're friends."

What a lie!

"Leonard tries so hard with Tamara, but she's constantly trying to turn him against me. She's still angry with her father, I think."

"She was two when it happened?" Mom asked, sympathetically.

Mrs. Luchio stared at Mom. "When what happened?"

75

"The car accident. Wasn't Tamara's father killed in a car accident?"

"Heavens, no. He's living in Los Angeles. He's a cameraman. To tell you the truth, I count my blessings he's no longer with us."

I could feel Mom's eyes looking at me, as if to say: *See? I told you your friend was lying!*

"Tamara seems to think her father's leaving is my fault." Mrs. Luchio kept talking between bites. "And then, when Saul, my boyfriend, left, Tamara wouldn't forgive me. Sometimes I blame myself for letting him spend so much time with her. It never occurred to her that he wouldn't stay."

I couldn't stand to hear any more. I felt stunned—had Tamara really lied or was Bette the liar?

I went into the kitchen to be by myself, but as soon as I'd sat down, I heard a knock on the door. Miguel stood next to me. "Hey, don't forget to invite me over."

"Are you leaving?"

"Yeah, I have to work."

For a minute we stood there awkwardly, me sitting, him standing, each of us waiting for the other to say something.

He studied my face. "Are you okay? Why are you sitting in here by yourself?"

"Tired, I guess," I whispered.

"Well . . ." He turned to leave. "Take it easy."

Then in my usual way, I had to say something stupid. "Thanks for everything," I said, which sounded way too formal.

"What are you thanking me for?" Miguel smiled. "It was your party. I should be thanking you." He winked. "Hey, thanks."

Mom knew I was upset and found me in the kitchen. "I like Mrs. Luchio very much. She's a very honest woman."

"Yeah, too honest. I thought she'd never stop spilling her problems about her horrible daughter, who happens to be my best friend. Don't you think it's strange she'd tell you all that stuff after she just met you?"

"Leah, you need to ask Tamara more questions. She's not being honest with you."

"Just like Tamara said—mothers always side with each other." I stood up. "Why are you trying to ruin my friendship with Tamara?"

"That's not what I'm telling you," Mom whispered, hugging me.

I shrugged off her hug.

"Leah"—Mom's voice grew soft—"I'm sure Tamara has her reasons for being so angry. But don't take all her stories for granted. A good friendship isn't a blind friendship, okay?"

"Just because Tamara's not as blunt as José's aunt," I said angrily.

"What do you mean?" Mom asked.

"She said they'd never allow a divorced woman in their family—she practically said you should give up on him."

Mom's face lost its smile. I was glad I'd hurt her, after what she'd done by inviting Tamara's mom over.

When José came in, Mom turned her back on him. "Your aunts weren't too subtle. I thought they'd never stop asking me about my divorce, my job, how in the world I could work and raise a child!"

José shrugged. "Don't worry about it—it's just their way."

"Mmmmm," Mom said. "Your mom barely spoke to me. Is that just her way?"

"She brought you a gift." José walked up and put his arms around Mom's waist from behind, while she ignored him and kept stacking the dishes.

"What's going on?" he asked. "I thought you'd be happy. We just gave our first party together, a very successful party!"

"Why didn't Miguel's parents come?" I asked.

"My brother and his wife, Miguel's parents, were killed in a car accident six years ago when Miguel was only nine. Now I'm his legal guardian until he turns eighteen."

I wondered why Mom hadn't mentioned Miguel to me before.

"You should come to our church and hear Miguel sing in the choir on Sundays." José said. "He does the solos—what a voice!"

Suddenly Mom turned and snapped, "Now you want to make me into a nice Catholic girl! Maybe you'd be better off with someone else. Someone your family could approve of!"

I knew it was time to make my exit, so I went to collect dirty glasses. Miguel in a choir, a church choir? As Tamara always said, what a mixture of weirdness boys are.

I waited until Mom and José had settled things in the kitchen, then I went in and asked Mom if I could leave.

"What about the dishes? We could use an extra pair of hands. . . ." José said.

"Be home by eight?" Mom asked.

I nodded.

I saw José look at her, questioning her, and I saw Mom nod, as if to say silently that she'd explain later. She must have known where I was going. She must have guessed that I had to find Tamara. I had to find out the truth.

13

Ever since Tamara fell for Caesar, her favorite place to hang out has been the Oriental Drugstore. Inside there's an old-fashioned soda fountain—a counter where you can sit and order the daily specials for $1.80 or malts and cheeseburgers. Tamara loves to sit there and watch people. When she's depressed, she orders a chocolate malt, which they serve in one of those huge tall malt-glasses, already chilled.

That's where I found her, eating her Thanksgiving dinner—a chocolate malt—at the Oriental Drugstore among all the people who had nowhere else to go.

When she saw me, she stared, without smiling. "Shouldn't you be at your party?"

"It's over." I took the stool next to her.

"So?" she asked.

"So?" I repeated.

"Did Bette make her grand entrance?"

I nodded and ordered a Coke. "My mother really liked your mom. They got along great."

Tamara looked down. "Everyone likes my mom. Because they don't have to live with her."

"Your mother had a good time."

"Telling everyone how difficult I am?" Tamara asked, facing me. "Isn't that what she discussed with your mom?"

I shrugged. "She just said you've had a really hard time."

Tamara refused to look at me. "And?"

"And what?" I asked.

Suddenly Tamara faced me. "Why don't you just say what you came to say, instead of pretending?" Her voice was sharp—like she was accusing me. She stared. "What are you waiting for me to say . . . you want me to apologize? Is that what you came for?"

Tamara's voice had risen, and people were watching us. "Okay," she hissed, "I'm sorry. There, now you can go."

I didn't know what to say. I'd come to talk, not fight. I'd wanted to tell her about Miguel . . . and ask her some questions about her dad, and find out her reason for telling me lies, since I was sure she had a good reason. But here we were, blaming each other, just because I'd found out the truth.

Tamara's eyes had tears in them, her voice was low. "Look at you, Miss Perfect. Perfect father, perfect mother. You spend winters with one, summers with the other. The truth is, the only reason people think you're so perfect is that you never talk. You just smile and listen. Perfectly obedient! That's what you are!"

80

I could barely breathe, my chest tightened so. "Tamara, you're the one with the beautiful apartment and your own water bed. And your mom who could have been Miss America! You're the one who gets to buy clothes whenever you want!"

"All Bette buys is my silence!" Tamara stared straight ahead, her voice controlled.

"What do you mean by that?" I whispered.

"Nothing. Except if my biggest problem was that my mom dated a guy like José, I'd be the happiest girl in this city."

"Tamara!"

"God, Leah, grow up! You don't live with a mother who's totally obsessed with looking young and staying young. I mean, everything with Bette is appearance. If I eat a cookie, she talks about my skin. If I drink milk, she talks about fats. No matter what I wear, Bette makes some criticism about the color, or she'll ask me if my clothes are tight because I'm gaining weight." Tamara turned and faced me. "My own mother has had her breasts done."

"She did?"

"Do you know what that means? She's got fake breasts. Hers weren't good enough. And you know what, my boobs are just like hers were—you know how that makes me feel?"

Tamara paused and shook her head. "When she has men over, she expects me to stay in my room. She doesn't want me hanging around because she says I flirt with them —she always thinks I'm after the guys she's after. It's absurd! That's why I have to act so rude . . . it's the only way to deal with Bette. So she can't accuse me of competing. You don't know how lucky you are!"

"Tamara, why are you mad at me? What'd I do?"

81

"Nothing. You never do anything—that's your problem!"

"Tamara! How can you say that! You're the one who lied!" I could feel other people stare at me as my voice rose, so I leaned over and whispered. "Now you're trying to make me feel bad because you . . . you always . . ."

"Always what?" Tamara asked coldly.

"Always lie so other people look bad, like nothing's your fault. You shouldn't have told me all those stories, especially since I told you the truth about José and Mom."

"Maybe you don't have as much to hide."

"Meaning what?"

Tamara faced me, and her voice wavered as she spoke. "Look, maybe I did make up some stuff, but not all of it. I mean, Bette's never killed anyone directly. But she did do something terrible, and I'm the only one who knows."

"See, Tamara? That's exactly what I mean. It's like you're always inventing things . . . stories . . . so I'll feel sorry for you. I'm sick of feeling sorry for you, especially when it's all a big, fat lie!"

"Why don't you just leave, then!" Tamara said loudly. "You're just like everyone else. I don't care if you believe me." She turned and laughed. "Anyway, you're not going to have to put up with me much longer . . . you might as well leave, now."

I draped my purse over my shoulder. "You can't stand it when people see through you, Tamara." I stood up and pulled on my hat and mittens.

Tamara turned around on her stool and snapped, "Yeah, well at least there's something to see through."

I began walking toward the cashier, but not before Tamara whispered loudly, "With you, it's all on the surface . . . no depth, nothing to see through!"

As I got farther from her, her voice got louder. "Clones!" The sound of her carried me into the night air, and then, surrounded by the noise of traffic and the bitter cold, I cried because I'd really come to find out why Tamara had lied, and I left not knowing if I even had a friend.

Despite my promise to Mom that I'd take the bus, I walked home alone, replaying the conversation in my mind, again and again, asking myself if I'd been too mean—or was I just being honest? Too honest, maybe? Did it even matter, if Tamara hated me?

When I tried to explain to Mom that I'd had a fight with Tamara and that's why I'd walked home, she just yelled at me.

"That's no excuse!" Mom was sitting at the table while José was drying dishes. "You always have an excuse for everything, Leah."

"What's your problem?" I asked her, glaring at José.

"Leah, don't talk to me like that. Don't you think girls your age disappear? Doesn't it sink in that girls like you are raped and murdered every day?"

I hate it when Mom starts lecturing. "So I'm never supposed to go outside?" I asked.

Mom shook her head. "Not after dark. Not alone. Not in this day and age."

I just stomped out of the kitchen, shaking my head, and when I got to the hallway, I whispered, "Bitch," loud enough for Mom to hear.

"Leah, come back here, right now!"

I slammed the door shut like I hadn't heard her.

83

Suddenly Mom pushed the door open and walked into my room. I'd never seen her look so mad.

"I want you to come back in there right now. We're going to talk this out."

"Talk what out?"

"Your problem!"

"I don't have a problem," I stated matter-of-factly. "You're the one with the problem. You've got José's whole family against you, and you're taking it out on me!"

Mom glared at me. "You're just like your father. You pretend nothing's wrong, then you vent your feelings on the people who love you most. Something happened between you and Tamara, and I want to know what! Why didn't she show up today?"

I shrugged. "I don't know. I couldn't find her tonight. Anyway, why should she come to your stupid party?"

"It looked like you were having a pretty good time talking to Miguel."

"Oh, sure," I said, mocking Mom. "All he did was talk about music, like he's the world's greatest gift to human ears. Or maybe he thinks his chest is some great gift to women, wearing his shirt open like that!"

José had entered and suddenly faced Mom. "You're too lenient with her. No one in my family would ever talk that way—they respect each other. I'm sick of letting her walk all over you . . . she's prejudiced and self-centered, and the fact that you let her get away with it makes me wonder why you're dating me!" José's voice had risen to yelling. "Why don't you act like a mother, instead of trying to be her best friend?" He turned to me. "And I'm sick of your snide remarks. Every day I work with kids who have it much harder than you, but they show a hell of a lot more character. If your mother allows you to talk that way to

84

her, fine. But don't ever, and I mean ever, let me hear you talk about my nephew that way. He's talented, all right, but more important than that, he's kind. Which is more than I can say for you."

José turned and left both Mom and me stunned. We heard the back door close, and José's car back out of the driveway. Mom started crying. Then she rose and walked out of my room, but turned before she closed the door. "Proud of yourself, Leah? Is this the way you wanted to end Thanksgiving?" She shook her head, like she was ashamed. "You can't live in separate worlds, one with your friends, one with me. Not until you're grown up and out of this house. Don't ever talk to me the way you did tonight—and don't ever insult my friends, especially José and his family, or you'll be grounded for months."

"So what?"

"And you won't visit your father spring break."

"You can't decide for Daddy, so don't even try. And if you do ground me, I'll just run away. This isn't the greatest family anymore, *sí señorita?*" I said, mocking José's voice.

"I didn't realize how mean you could be." Mom shook her head. "I didn't raise you to be prejudiced, it's somebody else's influence. Too bad you don't have the courage to be yourself."

Then she slammed the door before I could yell anything back.

Suddenly I hated everyone and everything. All I could do was lie down and wait, wait until I fell asleep and forgot who I was. I cried until I had to sit up to breathe. The truth was, I hadn't meant what I'd said, because I did like Miguel, and I hoped I'd get to see him again. But now José would tell him I was self-centered and prejudiced. And really, more than anything I wanted them to like me, all of

85

them. It seemed like no one really understood me, not the me inside. I'd blown it with everyone. Not even Tamara had trusted me enough to tell me the real truth. If there was such a thing as the real truth!

14

The next thing I knew, Mom was shaking me out of my sleep. "Honey, Mrs. Luchio's on the phone. Something terrible has happened. Tamara's run away. She never went home last night."

"You're kidding!" I smiled because I guess it just seemed so typical of Tamara, and also because I really didn't believe it.

"Mrs. Luchio wants to talk to you. Quick! She's waiting."

I ran to the phone, and the minute I heard her voice, I could tell Mrs. Luchio was really worried. "I got home last night from your house, and she hadn't been home all day. I waited up, but she never came in. The police insist on waiting longer. I don't know what else I can do. Leah, where would she have gone?

Suddenly I remembered what Tamara had said about not having to put up with her much longer. I should have known. I could have done something. It was probably my fault Tamara had run away. I'd walked out on her.

"Did you see her yesterday?" Mrs. Luchio asked.

"No," I said, afraid Mrs. Luchio would blame me if she knew the truth.

"Is there anyone at school who Tamara might have contacted?"

"We were best friends. There really wasn't anyone else we were close to."

"I was afraid of that," Mrs. Luchio said, which sort of hurt me, but then she added, "I was just hoping for a clue, someone she might have turned to."

Mrs. Luchio said she was going to call the police again and hire a private detective. She asked whether I would come over later in the day if Tamara didn't turn up.

"Please, Leah, if she calls, get in touch right away. Something could happen, sometimes terrible things happen to girls your age!"

"Did she have any money?" I asked.

"Yes, unfortunately. She'd been saving money for a long time, so she had a couple hundred dollars, plus she took my credit cards, which is probably a good thing. Once she starts charging things, we can trace her."

It still didn't seem real to me that Tamara was a runaway. And I couldn't imagine anything bad happening to her. But after I got off the phone, Mom started talking about child prostitutes and how men take them and use them in films to make money, and how the girls are drugged, so they don't even know where they are. Sometimes they die or get murdered.

I felt terrible. I thought of how Tamara dressed with belts and tight pants and all her makeup. Plus, she had a big chest which made her look older. If I were a man, I knew I'd go for Tamara.

Tamara didn't return home. Mrs. Luchio called around four and asked us to come over. I guess Mom knew I was pretty upset, because she offered to go to the Luchios' with me, which was nice because I really didn't want to go alone. Not that I don't like Mrs. Luchio and Jake, but I was feeling guilty about not having done anything to stop Tamara, and I was scared Mrs. Luchio would find out that I'd seen Tamara right before she left. Somehow I knew she'd blame me for not doing anything to stop Tamara.

I also thought of what Tamara had told me about Bette. "She really did do something terrible!" Tamara had said. Plus, the more I saw Mrs. Luchio, the more perfect she seemed. Too perfect! Maybe that's why I suddenly felt a little frightened of her myself.

When we got to their apartment, Jake was at basketball practice, so it was just the three of us. Mrs. Luchio served Mom some tea and me some juice, and then sat down across from us. She looked different. Her hair was braided down her back, and her face looked tired, maybe because she didn't have any makeup on, and her eyes were puffy underneath.

"I haven't slept all night," she said, more to Mom than me. "The police won't do anything for forty-eight hours, so I've called a private detective. Still, no one seems to think this is as serious as I do." Mrs. Luchio paused and drank some tea. "No one knows Tamara like I do. She's too smart

89

for her own good. That's why she gets herself into so much trouble."

Mom moved closer and took Mrs. Luchio's hand.

"It's so good of you to come over." Mrs. Luchio continued, "The detective will be here soon, and then Leah can tell us everything she knows."

I looked at Mom—how could I do that? How was I supposed to provide the clues and not let down my best friend?

Mom nodded, just slightly. "Honey, we have to think of Tamara's safety, above everything else."

The detective was a short, wiry man with gray hair. He smoked a pipe while he talked, which made him speak out of the corner of his mouth like Popeye. When I was introduced, he wrote my name on his pad of paper and said, "Okay, let's get started."

It was hard to think of things to say, because I knew so much. Was I supposed to tell them about the boys we liked, and where we wanted to go with them if they ever asked us out? I told them about Tamara's picture of the celebrities drinking champagne, and what she had said about José filling her in on California.

The detective turned to Mom and asked if José had ever talked to her, but Mom shook her head and glared at me. "They've never met. We've never met Tamara!"

I told them things I thought Tamara wouldn't mind my telling, but I said nothing about the previous day, the fight we'd had.

The detective smiled at me. "It's very important that you think hard and tell us if she gave you any clues, anything. When was the last time you saw her? What kind of mood was she in? Was there anyone else with her? What was she carrying—things like that. Any boyfriends?" the detective asked.

I told him about Caesar.

"More recent." The detective was staring at me. "When you last saw her, the exact time and place, what you talked about. All the details. . . ."

I looked at Mom, who nodded at me. "This is important, Leah. You've got to tell us everything, for Tamara's sake."

"Last time I saw her was Wednesday after school," I lied. "She was running toward her bus. She seemed the same as always."

"Did Tamara talk about her homelife?" the detective asked me. "Did she mention her mother? Or father?"

I didn't know what to answer. Of course she did. But with Bette sitting two feet away from me, and already upset, how was I supposed to tell him that Tamara called her mother a murderer?

That's when Mom came over and sat next to me. "Leah, no one's going to blame you. Tell everything."

Mrs. Luchio was about to cry. She kept shaking her head and blowing her nose into a Kleenex. I felt terrible. How could Tamara put me in this position?

"Well," I mumbled, "she talked about Mrs. Luchio. She called her Bette."

Mrs. Luchio gave a whimpery little laugh.

"She said . . ." I glanced at Mom, then at Mrs. Luchio, but I couldn't say anything.

Mom looked at the detective. "Tamara told Leah that her mother was a murderer. She said her mother had murdered her stepfathers by fixing them unhealthy food. I know it sounds crazy—" Mom spoke quickly like she wanted to get it over with.

"What?" Mrs. Luchio was shocked. "What!" Her voice grew shrill, "What stepfathers?"

The detective was busy scribbling on his pad. Mom and I glanced at each other, then we just stared at Mrs. Luchio.

"Well, since her dad . . ." I paused.

"You don't have to tell me!" Mrs. Luchio stated. "Ever since her father left, she's been lying about me." She started shaking her head back and forth, then laughed. "I should have known, that's why you invited us over for Thanksgiving. You wondered if I was a murderer. And that's why you were asking such strange questions." Mrs. Luchio glared at Mom. "After two kids her father discovered he didn't like marriage. That's the kind of man he is." She stood up and walked over to the window. "I can't believe this is happening. I should have seen it coming. Every time Tamara asks to visit her father, I call him up, and he says no way. He tells me he's got a project to finish and he can't take time off from work. He says he's not ready." She paused and blew her nose. "Tamara listened on the phone once last year—it crushed her."

"But what about all your boyfriends?" I blurted. "What about Saul? Didn't he die of heart failure?"

Mrs. Luchio nodded. "Yes, Saul died. And I'm sure Tamara twisted the truth around to make it seem as if his death was my fault. She has an amazing imagination!" She blew her nose. "After Tamara's father and I got separated, I had a boyfriend named Saul—Tamara adored him. She wanted a father and was always trying to impress him. He told Tamara he was going to marry me. But I didn't love him. Then after we broke up, he had a stroke, and at the funeral we talked with the doctor, a good friend, who told us that had Saul watched his diet, he could have lived much longer. Tamara somehow created a story that I had fed him foods that brought about his death! It's absurd."

"Leah"—the detective smiled at me—"did she say anything else about Jake or her mother?"

I shook my head.

Just then Jake came bursting in, sweaty and flushed from basketball practice. "Any news from El Freako, the runaway?"

Mom looked at me and raised her eyebrows. Mrs. Luchio introduced Mom and the detective to Jake, before he turned toward me. "Was Caesar in school today?"

I shrugged as if to say I didn't know.

"He wasn't at practice today," Jake continued. "She's been after him for weeks, so maybe they took off together. She lives to impress him!"

"She does not! She's only talked to him once," I stated.

"Well, that doesn't stop her from following him around. Did you tell them about the padlock and key?" Jake smiled at me.

I could feel my face turn red from anger, but I had never argued with a boy before. I couldn't think of anything to say.

Jake started laughing. "Did you mention three-alarm chili? Maybe we should go through the whole list!"

I felt like he'd just slapped me across the face. My face burned—how did he know about the list? That was Tamara's and my secret—our top secret!

Everyone was waiting for Jake to explain, but he just kept on laughing. "El Freako will do anything for attention. She's probably kidnapped Caesar just to get him to look at her!"

"I think we've heard enough," Mrs. Luchio snapped.

"Some of us are genuinely concerned about your sister, Jake. If you can't be serious, go into your own room."

Suddenly he was next to me, whispering in my ear. "You two have great phone conversations. I should have taped them and sold them. I could have made a mint."

Then out loud, so everyone, especially me, could hear, he said, "I'm so glad that I'm a tedious person. I'm so tedious I don't have to run away to get everyone to notice me."

"Enough, Jake." Mrs. Luchio was stern, glaring at him until he left the room.

My face burned, but not until we were in the car heading home could I let everything out. Tears streamed down my cheeks.

"Want to talk about it?" Mom asked. "I know Jake said something to really upset you."

How could I tell anyone about the list? Had Jake actually heard the whole conversation? I remembered the night Tamara told me over the phone about kissing Clay Smith. "Three-alarm chili." She'd giggled. "He's an incredible kisser!"

"Is it the same when you see Caesar?" I had asked her.

"Two-alarm chili!"

We went through a whole list of guys in our classes, and if they turned us on, we'd say chili, and if they were duds, we'd say turkey vegetable.

Driving home Mom didn't say much, except as we were turning into the driveway. "I'm glad I'm not Bette Luchio —she's got her hands full with Jake and Tamara. I guess I lucked out to have you for a kid, huh?"

I smiled but said nothing.

"Are you okay?" Mom tried to hug me, but as soon as we were inside the house, I escaped to my room. I knew

Mom felt bad. She thought I was still hurt because Tamara had lied to me. She didn't know I was lying, too, lying because I didn't want Mom and Mrs. Luchio to know that it was my fault Tamara had run away.

That's why I felt bad, because maybe Tamara did have something to hide, something that was too awful to admit . . . and I hadn't even given her a second chance to explain.

15

On the Monday after Thanksgiving vacation Tamara didn't show up for school. I ate lunch by myself, a soggy tunafish sandwich that had been fermenting in a locker for six hours. I was lonely. Without Tamara around I didn't have anyone else to talk to.

I was exhausted by the time I got home, so I took the phone, which has a very long extension cord, and a bag of cookies into my room. I called Tamara's place, but there was no answer. Then I had a cookie attack. Sometimes I get like that, like I can't stop eating cookies, usually when I'm depressed. I eat until whatever I'm eating is gone. I felt so stuffed and sick to my stomach, I had to lie down.

I'd been thinking about two things all day—Tamara's

gone, and Miguel's never going to call because José has probably already told him I'm prejudiced and self-centered.

I couldn't decide if José was still mad. He'd been over most of the weekend and he'd been somewhat friendly, though not his old self. I apologized to him for saying what I had, and Mom seemed to forgive and forget, but José had been more distant. I got the feeling he didn't trust me anymore.

So there I was on my bed, having porked out until a entire box of Girl Scout Savannahs began to erode the inside of my stomach, half of me trying to stay hopeful about a guy, the other half morbid about my best friend, when the phone rang.

At first I hoped it was Miguel, then I wished it would be Tamara. My stomach expanded as I sat up and caught the phone on the second ring. "Hello?"

I listened for a voice, but there was nothing, just some static on the line.

"Hello?"

More silence. Somehow, through the silence, I thought I heard breathing, female breathing, but I wasn't sure. Seconds passed, and I listened to the breathing, trying to figure out the noise in the background. Could it be Tamara, I wondered.

"Hello . . ." I repeated. "Tamara?"

Then I heard the click. Whoever was on the other line had hung up. Deep down my instincts told me it was Tamara. But why wouldn't she talk to me? Did she think I'd tell on her? Or get mad at her? Or was she frightened of something or someone and couldn't talk?

I debated whether to tell Mom, but decided against it, not unless it happened again. After all, it could've been a prank caller, some kid who got bored after school.

97

But it did happen again. Tuesday after school, just as I walked in the door, there was another phone call—silence, even as I spoke into the phone, just silence.

"Is that you?" I whispered. "Are you in trouble?"

Silence.

"Tamara, if it's you, please talk to me."

Still no voice answered me.

"Tamara, if this is supposed to be funny, please don't do it. Tell me if you're okay. Please!"

I heard something, a gulp or a gasp, as if she were holding her breath, maybe holding back tears, or was it laughter?

"Tamara?" I asked softly, my spine suddenly prickling with doubts.

Click.

I had chills running up my back. It had to be Tamara, but why would she do that to me? Why would she remain silent?

Wednesday, Mom and José were in the kitchen. I was waiting when the phone rang, but Mom got to it first.

"Hello?" she asked. "Hello?" Mom paused, as though listening, then hung up. "Wrong number, I guess."

Thursday I waited, and when the call came, I asked only once, "Tamara?" Immediately the line went dead. It had been a week since Tamara had run away, a week since I had heard her voice.

The next day I waited again. My frustration with Tamara's silence was growing. I couldn't imagine why she would continue to call, only to hang up on me without saying a single word.

The phone rang and this time I picked it up and listened, without saying anything into the receiver. I thought maybe she'd ask if I was there, listening. Instead, no one spoke for several seconds, but for the first time I heard rock music in the background.

"Where are you?" I finally whispered.

The only reply was the expected click. That's when I decided to tell Mom. A week of silent phone calls was too weird, even for Tamara.

"Mom," I whispered, as she sat watching TV, "I've got something to tell you."

Mom nodded.

"Something you're not going to like."

José came into the room and set down a tray with grilled cheese sandwiches and iced tea. "Is this private or can I be here?" he asked.

"You can stay." I went over and turned down the sound on the TV. "I lied to you . . . and Mrs. Luchio . . . and Detective Grey."

Mom waited for me to continue.

"It's my fault Tamara ran away. I called her a liar."

"I thought you must have seen her." Mom sighed. "Tell us the whole story."

So I did. I told them we'd had a fight, and Tamara had hinted that I'd never see her again, and still I'd left her there. "It never occurred to me that she would really go to California. It's probably my fault she left."

"Leah"—Mom's voice was soft—"Tamara did lie. You had a right to be angry. But you should've told us. We might have caught up to her by now—who knows what kind of trouble she's in?"

"One more thing," I whispered. "I think she's been calling me every day."

"What! And you didn't say anything to us?" Mom yelled.

"I'm not sure if it's Tamara. It's just that every day we

get a phone call after I get home from school, and as soon as I start asking questions, asking if it's Tamara, the phone goes dead."

Mom closed her eyes. "God, what if she's in trouble, real trouble. Does it sound long distance?"

I nodded.

"Leah, I'm really upset you didn't say anything to me. She might be phoning for help, but for some reason she can't speak!"

"But I promised Tamara never to tell our secrets. I didn't know what to do!"

"That's ridiculous!"

"Wait a minute, Jessica." José's voice was calm. "In some ways the phone calls are a good sign—we know she's alive, right?"

I shivered.

"And Leah probably hoped Tamara would talk eventually, right? Anyway, we aren't sure if it is Tamara, though if the calls are long distance, it's probable."

"Well, I'm calling Bette Luchio right now." Mom stood up. "She's got to know this as soon as possible."

"I don't have to talk to her, do I?"

"I think you should apologize," Mom said.

"Why not wait?" José intervened. "Leah can apologize later when things have settled down."

I only heard Mom's side of the conversation, but even so, I knew Mrs. Luchio was furious.

"Yes . . . I'm terribly sorry. . . . Leah didn't mean to, she thought she was being a good friend. . . . Well, I'm sorry you feel that way. . . . Of course we want to see Tamara back alive and safe. . . . No, Leah meant her no harm, my daughter would never intentionally hurt Tamara. . . . She feels terrible, she'd like to apologize at another

time. . . . Well if that's how you feel, I'm sorry. . . ."
Mom slammed down the phone.

"If I had Bette Luchio for a mother, I might run away too!" Mom sat down. "She had the audacity to say that she expected such behavior from a girl like you."

I sat, stunned. I'd thought Mrs. Luchio had liked me.

An hour later we received a phone call from the telephone company. The representative asked Mom to make a record of all the phone calls from the last week and continue to keep a list of the prank calls for the next five days in order to establish a pattern. The representative announced that on Monday the company would be putting a tracer on the phone to locate the caller.

"They aren't prank calls," Mom insisted. "They're just silent calls. Probably from my daughter's best friend."

"Silent phone calls which occur daily are a form of harassment and are treated as such," the representative told Mom.

Mom hesitated, but agreed to accommodate the phone company, since it apparently was Detective Grey's idea. He called immediately after the phone company, and told Mom that Monday he'd be over to tape the call himself, in case there was some way of locating her rapidly by magnifying the sounds.

I felt terrible—what if Tamara was just calling to check in? What if the phone calls were her method of maintaining our friendship, our secret code? Maybe I should warn her so she could stop phoning. But then we'd lose contact, and what if she was in real trouble?

"Tamara shouldn't put us through all this," Mom stated afterward. "I wonder if she has any idea how worried everyone is."

"Mom, it's just as much your fault as Tamara's!"

101

"My fault!" Mom glared. "I've never even met her." She turned to José. "I've never met this girl who's controlling our lives."

"Yeah," I mumbled. "And if you hadn't forced the issue, we never would have met Mrs. Luchio, and Tamara wouldn't have felt like a fool, and I wouldn't have fought with her and called her a liar."

"Leah, you can blame me for a lot of things. But don't try to blame me for Tamara's behavior. You're blaming other people instead of facing your own anger and disappointment. It's not my fault Tamara let you down."

"You don't have to defend Tamara," José whispered to me.

Tears clouded my eyes.

"Take it easy, okay?" José gave my arm a pat.

Seeing how nice he was made me think of Miguel. All week I'd waited for a phone call from him, but I'd heard nothing. Not only had I lost my best friend, but it seemed I'd also lost my first chance at a boyfriend too.

16

The phone calls kept coming, and each day I listened to the silence on the other end, my stomach knotting before, during, and after each phone call. Listening to Tamara's breathing, I wondered why she wouldn't talk to me. I wondered, too, what she'd do when she found out her calls were being traced.

Monday the detective arrived and set up a machine to tape the call. At exactly four o'clock, when the phone rang, he sat staring at me while I picked up the receiver. I was supposed to nod if it was the same kind of call that had been coming every day. I felt sick to my stomach as I nodded, listening to the silence that was being taped. "Tamara?" I asked, each breath tightening inside my chest.

I hated the detective, his blank expression. I hated the

way his mouth continued to suck on his pipe while the silence was collected on tape. My instructions had been to keep her on the line as long as possible, but I knew, from experience, the length of silence was totally unpredictable.

"Tamara, just tell me you're okay."

The detective nodded at me to keep asking questions.

"Tell me where you are, Tamara. Just tell me where you are!"

But it was too late. The line clicked dead, and the detective just glared at me as if I hadn't done my job.

All week I continued to feel nervous. I often dreamt the phone was ringing, and I'd wake up, knowing something was terribly wrong. During the day I couldn't stand to be by myself, but I also couldn't stand to be with Mom and José because they were constantly asking me if I wanted to talk about it—it being Tamara's departure.

"It's hard to feel abandoned." Mom would pour on the sympathy. "Want to talk about it?"

José tried a different tactic. "How about getting your mind off it? Want to go to the movie with us?"

The problem was, I didn't like being around José, because then I thought about Miguel, and I felt I had to be on my best behavior to make up for the stupid way I'd acted before.

Mom got pushy. "You never go out anymore, or see your other friends, Leah. Why don't you call Rachel?"

I didn't want to see anyone, because everyone from our school had heard about Tamara, and I could tell from the way people looked at me in the hallway, they wanted to ask me questions.

On Wednesday night Detective Grey called to inform Mom that Tamara had purchased a plane ticket to Los Angeles. Which is where, he confided, they'd located the originating point of the phone calls. Unfortunately, he told Mom, he was not at liberty to reveal more about the situation. He said they'd also talked to Tamara's father, who had given Tamara money to come home, which she apparently had used for other purposes. The detective and Mrs. Luchio were going to California over the weekend to find her.

"What's that supposed to mean?" I asked Mom. "What did he mean by 'other purposes'?"

She shook her head. "Who knows? He's being intentionally vague."

The day he was leaving for California, Detective Grey stopped by to see if there was any new information, and after we gave him the list of silent phone calls, Mom did her best to get rid of him quickly. "Anything else?" Mom asked. "I'm sorry to seem in a rush, but we have guests coming for dinner, and I have to run to the store first."

Mom led him to the door.

"Thank you," he said curtly, letting the door slam behind him.

"You're not a good liar, Mom." I grabbed an apple. "He knew you were making up the story about dinner guests."

"I would never lie to the good detective." Mom rolled her eyes. "We are having guests. José's coming."

"You implied multiple guests."

"José's bringing someone."

I knew by the way Mom turned her back to me that something was up.

"Who?"

"Miguel."

"Miguel! Couldn't you have asked me first?"

"I knew you'd say no. You're becoming withdrawn. You've been nothing but a hermit for two weeks, so I thought I'd invite someone your age, and Miguel was the

105

logical choice. I've been wanting to get to know him better myself."

"Look at me, Mom. I haven't washed my hair. I don't have anything to wear."

"Leah, you look fine. Treat him like a friend. José's family is very informal. Trust me."

"What am I supposed to talk to him about?"

Mom sighed impatiently. "Look, you don't have to talk to him if you don't want to. I will. Anyway, I asked him to bring his guitar and play for us. José says he's the best guitarist in town."

"Well, I'm sure there's no bias involved in that judgment."

"Go take a shower." Mom pushed me out of the kitchen. "You'll feel better."

It was weird when José and Miguel arrived. José kissed Mom and Miguel hugged her. Then Miguel put down his guitar case and shook my hand. That was the weird part. He just stuck out his hand like a robot, so I stuck out mine.

Then we all sat down at the table and proceeded to stuff ourselves on Mom's lasagna. José and Miguel did most of the talking and told us all about their family history.

"The men in our family are either priests or teachers," José said. "It's either/or . . . those are the only two professions that go over big with the matriarchy, my mother!"

"What did your father teach?" Mom asked Miguel.

"Music. He was a composer and music teacher. He taught classical guitar." Miguel told us about his father's career. "He always wanted to perform, but he had to do more teaching to support us."

106

Finally after we'd all finished, Mom stood up. "I can't wait any longer. While I let the ice cream thaw, let's hear you play."

I thought we'd have to beg him to play, but Miguel wasn't the least bit shy. "What do you want to hear?" he asked, as he started tuning the strings. He looked at me, and right in front of Mom and José, he said, "Leah, what would you like to hear—the first one's your choice!"

I felt embarrassed, sitting across from a guy close to my own age who was going to perform for me.

"Well?" he asked. "What kind of music do you like?" He was leaning back with his feet on the coffee table, his guitar resting on his thigh. I was in the chair opposite him, my mind blanking out all the songs I'd ever heard. I noticed other things, the way his jeans tightened across his thighs, showing his leg muscles, and the way his shirtsleeves were rolled up, so his arms flexed when he moved his hand to make chords. But right at that moment I couldn't think of the name of one song—not one.

"Okay," he said, as if I'd answered his question, "if you know the lyrics to any of these, you have to promise to sing along."

Sure, I thought, *me sing with you, right out loud.*

Then suddenly I was listening to this guy practically my own age who could really sing, like a professional. I mean, he could hit high notes and low notes, and he didn't seem to mind singing out loud, really loud, so that his voice filled the whole room. Each time he'd finish, we applauded. He played classical music, jazz, even an old Beatles tune.

After several songs he put down his guitar and smiled at Mom. "Isn't the ice cream thawed?"

"Hearing you play made me forget—you're incredible, really incredible!" Mom said.

107

"Yeah, you are," I added.

"Thanks."

As soon as dessert was over, Mom announced that she and José were going to a movie. "Want to come?"

But Miguel had seen the movie, so we stayed at our house. As soon as they left, he picked up his guitar again and sang a beautiful lullaby about an owl that watched over a baby when it sleeps. When he finished, I asked him if that was one of the songs he'd written himself.

"No, my father wrote that. He taught me how to play." Miguel kept strumming as he talked.

"Do you miss him?" I whispered. "Do you miss your mom and dad?"

Miguel hesitated. "Sometimes. But always it's when I least expect it. The accident is like a blur, like someone poured water over a photograph, and no one will be able to see the real picture ever again. You know? They say kids remember things like that, but I don't. I only remember their voices right before the accident. I was sitting in the backseat, and they were laughing up front. That's all I remember."

I sat there listening, not knowing what to say. Something about Miguel's voice held me still inside.

"Sometimes I feel like crying for no reason." He laughed sadly. "It's not the sanest way to live."

I'd never had a boy talk to me like that, showing his real feelings and everything. I wanted to go over and touch Miguel, put my arm on his shoulder or something, but I couldn't. I kept looking at his lips, wondering how it would feel to kiss him. Then I'd feel my face blush, wondering, too, if he knew what I was thinking.

"Hey, I didn't mean to bring you down. I try not to think about them so much anymore."

108

"It must be hard, though," I said. "Not to think about them. But at least you have José."

Miguel laughed. "José and I are really different—he's very old fashioned."

"José?"

"Yeah. He's okay, it's just that sometimes he's too free with advice, and most of his advice is outdated."

Miguel put his guitar back in his case. "Let's watch TV or something, all right?"

I turned on the TV and found a movie. The problem was we sat too far apart on the couch. Then, when this commercial came on about making sure you have your breath mints when you're on a date, Miguel started laughing. I wanted to laugh, too, but I felt embarrassed, like he could see right through me, see that I wanted him to kiss me. I waited to see if he was going to grab me during the commercial, but all he did was laugh.

Most of the girls I knew had been kissing for years. I was about the only one who'd never had a real boyfriend. Following Tamara's advice, I'd practiced kissing by putting a cup over my mouth and moving my tongue along the inside rim, making sure not to let too much saliva accumulate and keeping my mouth relaxed.

Suddenly Miguel went over and turned the channel to the music video station. "Let's dance," he whispered, extending his arm in my direction.

"Here?" I asked. "Just us?" At first I thought he was joking. But he started moving his hips and grabbed my arm at the same time. His movements were so natural, his hips and arms gripping the music, his body changing styles of dance, while I kept doing the same step that I'd practiced in the bathroom a thousand times. I avoided his eyes, though I knew he was watching me.

109

"This is stupid," I said, stopping.

"Don't you like to dance?"

I nodded. "But not alone."

"You're not alone." He grabbed me then and put his arms around my waist. "We just need a slower song." And he kissed my lips, just barely, and held me close so that I could feel his body keeping time, moving my body with his.

I loved being close—I could feel his heart when I put my cheek against his chest. I smelled the scent of his soap and the touch of his breath on my forehead. Most of all I felt the heat from his skin, from both our bodies touching.

We'd only slow-danced a couple of songs, when we heard Mom and José drive up. Miguel looked at me and laughed. "You dance okay," he whispered. "But I'll have to keep giving you lessons."

I knew he meant it to be nice, as a way of saying he wanted to see me again, but I felt stupid at the same time because I was an awful dancer, especially in front of him.

"Well, I better be going." Miguel grabbed his coat as soon as they walked in the door. "The choir has to rehearse tomorrow. Thanks."

José and Miguel left together while I stood there in the doorway with Mom. "Well?" Mom whispered. "You two have a good time?"

"It was okay." I didn't want Mom to know how much I liked Miguel because I knew she'd tell José.

Afterward, as I was brushing my teeth, I looked at my face in the mirror. It seemed okay, not beautiful like Tamara's, but all right. Mom always said I have a gentle face, Dad's Norwegian cheekbones and blond hair, and Mom's Danish gray eyes. But nothing special. I knew the guys would never drool over me. Still, I hoped what

Grandma always said was true—that I was attractive in a sophisticated way.

I lay there in bed for a long time, listening to the trucks on the highway about a mile away—it seemed strange how far the sound carried in the middle of the night. I wondered if maybe Tamara was lying awake too. I would have loved to tell her about Miguel—the way his arms felt. I couldn't sleep, even though it was close to three A.M. My body was wide awake with the feelings he'd left behind.

Suddenly a siren sounded, and then next door the dog started barking. Somewhere in the middle of all that noise, one thought kept coming into my mind. We all lose people. And then we're left with a certain silence, where their voices used to be. Like Miguel missing his parents.

That seemed important suddenly. I remember Grandma, after Grandpa died, used to blow him kisses on the wind. And now Miguel played songs for his parents. When Miguel had talked about his father, how he missed him, I had felt Tamara's absence—in some ways she'd been closer to me than anyone, even if she had lied. I listened to the wind rattle the screen. A few minutes later, when the wind turned to rain, I imagined Tamara was answering me, telling me she missed me too.

17

Two weeks ago Tamara ran away, two weeks ago today. When I got home from school, I was shocked to find a postcard from her. On the front was a picture of a blond, muscular lifeguard who was standing on a beach, flexing his muscles. He had on this little bikini-style bathing suit that showed everything. On the back Tamara wrote a little note. *Not bad, huh? Maybe I'll bring one home for you too. T.* That's all there was, just a *T,* and next to it, a smiley face. She'd put that on the back because we used to joke about how much we hated smiley faces.

When I showed the postcard to Mom, she insisted I call Bette and tell her about it, especially since it had been postmarked in Los Angeles, where Tamara's father lives.

"Mom, they've put a tracer on our phone. They must already know where she is."

"Leah, we don't want to repeat our mistakes."

Jake answered the phone and told me that Bette was in California with Detective Grey. "She sent a postcard to us four days ago," Jake added. "It had only one line that said, *I love you, sorry.* Jake laughed sarcastically. "Weird, huh? El Freako knows how to make the drama last—I'll give her that. Let's just hope this is the last act, not that I'm looking forward to seeing her."

I hung up without saying good-bye.

Tamara's silent phone call came thirty seconds later, the last I heard from her for a long time.

Mom stood in the hallway watching me as I put down the receiver. "Aren't you angry with her, for putting you through this?"

"I'm angry at myself. I shouldn't have told on her. For all we know she's happier there than at home."

Mom rolled her eyes. "Why don't you let Tamara take responsibility for her own actions?"

"What makes you think running away isn't taking responsibility for her own life?"

I had this feeling Mom was going to spend the entire weekend trying to cheer me up. And I couldn't stand waiting for the phone to ring, waiting for Miguel to call. So, out of complete desperation, I decided to go to Rachel Spencer's house.

As soon as we were settled on her bed, Rachel started in on the one subject I didn't want to discuss. "I don't know what you see in her," Rachel said. "I mean, Tamara's so"—she looked at the ceiling as though trying to locate the perfect word—"so . . . different."

"How profound," I mumbled.

113

Rachel smiled, opening a bag of Cheez Curls. Even though her parents are doctors, they always have tons of junk food around. We were sitting in Rachel's room, where everything matched, the old-fashioned canopy bed, desk and dresser, even a makeup table with special drawers for hairpins and perfume. Everything, the curtains and spread, were in different shades of blue, so it blended.

Rachel also kept bringing the conversation back to Tamara, like she wanted to find out information. "Isn't her mother some kind of health freak?"

I sat cross legged on her bed and just shrugged. "I don't know her very well. But she's the most beautiful woman I've ever seen."

Rachel squinted at me.

"She looks just like Tamara," I added.

"You think Tamara's pretty?" Rachel gasped and coughed, trying to be funny. "With that makeup and those clothes? It's like she's always trying to prove something."

I picked up a magazine and began reading it.

"Mom says girls who dress like that are really insecure!" Rachel continued.

"Tamara isn't insecure!" I said. "She's creative!" I could feel my face turning red. "She ran away because she hates it here. Just wait, she'll do something really spectacular with her life—that's the way Tamara is!"

"Oh, sure, like sell jewelry in Woolworth's—that's the kind of stuff she wears, ultracheap. You can always tell the kinds of girls who run away."

"Right, like you know everything about everything."

Rachel turned away from the mirror and faced me. "The sleazy ones, the ones who don't care about themselves —Mom says those are the ones who run away."

"Your mom's wrong," I told her angrily.

"Did you hear about the phone calls?" Rachel asked. "There's a rumor around school they've already tracked her down, by tapping phones. You were the only person who could put up with her, so you must know about that, right?"

"Where'd you hear that?"

Rachel smiled slyly. "Jake."

"What else did he say?"

"Nothing. Mrs. Luchio's away, looking for her spectacular daughter, and Jake's having a party this weekend. He called to ask me—aren't you going?"

I wondered if anyone besides me really missed Tamara.

"Tell me, did Tamara take her chain and padlock?" Rachel started laughing.

I just sat there, glaring at Rachel until she changed the subject.

"Who do you want to go to the Christmas dance with?" she asked.

"No one."

"Oh, come on, you must like someone!" Rachel said.

I thought of Miguel. If I asked him, he might wear something weird like a shiny shirt or his pointy shoes—it wouldn't be worth it. All the guys at my school wear the same thing—khakis or Levi's with a sport coat. Anything else would stand out.

"Well?" Rachel persisted. "Who?"

I shook my head.

"Look," Rachel whispered, "the only reason you never get asked out is that you're overly tall and overly smart. Mom says you'll be a late bloomer."

Rachel has this way of saying things that leave me speechless, because the hurt is so much larger than words.

115

"Leah, I meant that as a compliment. I just don't think you should worry if you don't get asked out."

"Thanks for your concern!" I got up and walked out of Rachel's room. No one was home, so I didn't worry about her parents hearing me. I just grabbed my coat and walked out the front door. I felt good inside because I knew Rachel hated to be alone in her house, and now she was sitting there probably scared to death, since it was getting dark outside. That'll show her, I thought.

But all the way home I kept hearing what Rachel had said, and it scared me. I loved Tamara, but it did seem like there was this line that people, mostly girls, could cross over, and after that, everyone stopped liking them.

The way Tamara dressed and acted, she would always be on the other side of the line, and I guess, when I decided I liked Tamara more than Rachel, that put me on the outside too. The problem was, you had a better chance of getting a guy if you were part of a group. I mean, school's just made up of groups, and if you don't stick with one, forget it. There are the preps, jocks, stuck-ups, and the fried chickens. Most of the fried chickens wear their hair shaved around their ears and get high a lot. Then there are the high-ons, like Jake. But the worst are the rejects—the nerds, the druggies, or the girls who sleep around and get a reputation. Boy preps date girl preps, and the male jocks date the female jocks, and if you aren't in a group, like Tamara and me, then you're invisible, and the invisibles end up mixing together or disappearing.

The only time the groups really mix is in gym class. There's a girl named Lynn Glickens, she's one of the best girl athletes—a soccer player. She always chooses the rejects and burnouts to be on her team, even though she's preppy

116

and could choose anyone. Rachel always whispers, "There goes the social worker!"

But Lynn's team wins sometimes. And it's always great to see somebody as popular as Rachel beat her. In the end of the semester competition Lynn and Rachel were both captains. Unfortunately Rachel picked me first and named our team the Ghosts. Our motto was We're too fast to be seen.

Lynn's team called themselves the Rescue Squad. ("How apropos," Rachel snickered. "Those girls need rescuing.") Their motto was We rescue the ball and answer the call—win, win!

The best part was that Lynn's team never even let us score, which I didn't mind at all, since Rachel was the captain, and I could see her getting more upset each time Lynn, who played goalie, rescued the ball.

"You're home early," Mom said, as I walked in the door.

"Brilliant deduction," I stated.

"You two had a fight?"

"The next time Rachel asks me over," I said, "remind me that I'm never that desperate."

"What happened?"

"Nothing."

"Did it have to do with Tamara?"

"Mom!" I glared at her. The last thing I wanted to do was talk.

"Well, if it makes you feel any better, Miguel called."

"He did? When?"

"Earlier. He wanted to see if you could go to a movie."

"What'd you say?"

117

"He asked if you were home and said he was calling to see if you wanted to go to a movie, after he got off work. I told him you were at a friend's house, and I offered to give him Rachel's number, but he said he'd call back later." Mom smiled at me. "You suddenly look cheered up."

"Yeah!"

Mom shook her head. "I thought you didn't like people like José . . . he and Miguel dress similarly, and—"

I interrupted. "Mom, José's fat. Miguel's handsome."

"So you're not prejudiced against Mexicans, you're just prejudiced against heavy people."

"I've grown to like José, okay?"

"Now that you've met Miguel."

"Okay, so I made a mistake when I first met José." I sat down across from Mom. "Why didn't you tell me about Miguel when you first introduced me to José?"

Mom looked at her empty soup bowl and smiled. "You aren't the only one who has difficulties accepting differences. José's mom would prefer a Catholic, a Mexican, and a woman young enough to have lots of children. Given her preferences I'd be her last choice. So we decided to keep our relationship quiet until we knew each other better."

"What does that have to do with Miguel?"

"José was afraid Miguel would say something to Mrs. Santiago, so he didn't want me to spend too much time with him. I didn't want you asking questions before I was ready to answer them, so we kept our relationship private on both sides."

"Now that you've come out of the closet, does that mean you're serious?"

"It means we're considering getting serious." Mom watched for my reaction."

"Would that make me related to Miguel?"

118

Mom turned and leaned over the sink, washing her hands. "You sound more serious than me." She laughed.

Only, there was something about her tone and the sharpness of her laughter, something that kept her from looking at me, that made me know her words weren't true —Mom was getting very serious about José.

18

That evening we had the first snow of the season. The falling flakes turned our entire backyard white. I liked to see the snow so smooth, without any tracks, just slopes of snow where the wind hit and made a sculpture out of the white powder. The woman upstairs who owns our house and rents us the basement apartment was playing the piano, practicing one line over and over again. I lay on my bed wishing Miguel would call back, so I could put on my new jacket and walk in the snow with him.

Mom and José were in the kitchen laughing, which made me feel lonelier than ever. I heard a knock on my door, and José invited me to taste the wassail—that's a drink he makes out of fruit juices and wine. "It's very healthy," he said, for my benefit.

Mom was making Christmas cookies, and I could smell the sweet scent of dough baking. Hearing them laugh together made me want someone of my own, so I wouldn't have to spend Saturday nights with them.

"No, thanks," I yelled back.

Then I heard the phone ringing, and judging by Mom's voice, it was someone she knew. Probably Rachel calling to apologize.

"Leah! It's Miguel."

I ran to the hallway and pulled the phone into my room, so I could talk without them hearing.

"Hello . . ."

"Leah, this is Miguel, how're you doing?"

"Fine. How are you?"

"Don't ask. I had to work tonight, and I'm supposed to work all day tomorrow too."

I tried to hide my disappointment, and ended up sounding like a female robot. "Sounds like you're pretty busy."

"Well, I have tomorrow night off, how about a movie?"

"Yeah, that'd be great."

"I hate to ask this, but could you meet me at Century Hall at six-thirty? I mean, I'd like to come by your house, but I don't get off work until then, and most of the movies start around seven."

"Fine. Mom can give me a ride."

"One more thing," Miguel said. "Grandma wants to know if you and your mom can come for dinner Christmas Eve . . . before Christmas Mass. It'll just be the five of us. The rest of the family doesn't come until Christmas Day."

When I asked Mom, I was surprised to see her roll her eyes, right in front of José, who whispered, "You don't have to go to Mass, don't worry!" Mom mumbled okay, so I told

121

Miguel I'd see him tomorrow night, and we'd put the dinner date on our calendar.

Century Hall, the place where Miguel works, is a huge old mansion that's been renovated with a stage and dance floor built onto the back behind the restaurant. When I walked in the front door, the guy asked to see my ID.

"Come on, sweetheart, you don't expect me to believe you're eighteen." He reached out his hand, palm flat. "Show some ID."

"I'm here to see Miguel."

"Miguel who?"

"Miguel Santiago, the guy who works in the kitchen."

The man nodded and smiled. "Tell the bartender, she'll get him." He let me pass. The place was filled with smoke and the smell of beer. There were so many people waiting to get drinks, it was hard to get close to the bar. The bartender, a blond-haired woman with lots of makeup, wore a shiny purple silk shirt and tight jeans. I stood near the corner of the bar until I could get her attention, then I yelled out, "Could you tell Miguel I'm here? Please?"

She smiled and nodded, looking me over head to toe, then picked up the telephone and pushed a button. "Hey, Bud, tell lover boy someone's here to see him."

Miguel was smiling when he came through the swinging doors. "Hi." He turned to the bartender. "Hey, Sheila, can you pay me cash tonight?"

Teasing, she batted her eyelashes. "Anything for you."

He looked at me and rolled his eyes. "She's all right, she likes to give me a hard time. She went out with José in high school."

I looked again. "José went out with her?" I whispered.

122

Miguel nodded. "He used to be wild—ran with a gang from the neighborhood."

"José?" I couldn't believe it. "When did he change?"

"After high school."

"Here." Sheila handed him two tens. "Tomorrow, nine o'clock, Miguel. Lock up when you're finished sweeping, okay?"

"Thanks, Sheila," Miguel said. We made our way out of the bar, and as we walked to the movie theater, Miguel held my hand, fingers entwined. He not only insisted on paying for the tickets, but also on buying popcorn. "Next time," he whispered, when I pulled open my purse and offered to pay my share.

Once we got to our seats, he put his arm around me, pulling me close. "You smell nice," he whispered, "like lemons."

Throughout the movie I snuggled next to him, so that every time he shifted his position, shifted his touch, I grew warmer inside.

It happened. Just as we got off the bus near my house, Miguel finally gripped my arms and pulled me close to him. Then gently, just as I had imagined, his mouth covered mine. A real kiss. A couple of seconds passed, then he took my hand and started walking toward my house. Neither of us knew what to say, so we just walked silently. Then, when we reached the porch, he kissed me again. The snow gleamed in the streetlights and everything was silent, except for the sound of someone shoveling snow somewhere down the block. His lips were so soft and his arms so tight—I didn't want him to stop.

"Want to come inside?" I asked.

Miguel looked toward the house. The lights were still on. "Maybe another night." He squeezed my hand tightly.

123

I had always heard that boys were supposed to lose control and want to do as much as possible as fast as they can, and girls are supposed to set limits. But Miguel was doing just the opposite—he was the one who was moving slowly. I didn't want him to go yet, I wanted to kiss more. Every time he touched me, my body shivered. Did it always feel this good, I wondered.

Miguel draped his arms around me and stared into my eyes. I'd never imagined such dark eyes as his. He kissed my lips, my forehead, then shifted positions so his whole body was touching mine. I could feel his chest as his arms circled me, squeezing tightly.

"Tonight's just right," he whispered. I watched him turn and walk quickly toward the bus stop, and I liked it, that he didn't say good-bye.

19

Miguel called both Sunday and Monday nights, which was especially nice, because I was anxious to talk to someone about Tamara. I'd expected a phone call from the Luchios, since Bette Luchio had been gone all weekend, but we still hadn't heard anything.

When I'd started to call their apartment on Sunday night, Mom told me to wait, let them call us. But when I saw Jake at his locker on Tuesday, I couldn't stand it any longer.

"Jake, have they found Tamara yet?"

I expected for him to say no. I guess I thought that if they had already found her, they would've let me know, or at least Tamara would have called.

His smile grew twisted and he nodded toward his

locker, without looking at me. "They found her, all right. But not in time."

I stood paralyzed, waiting. "What!"

"Not in time to keep her from ruining herself. You'd probably enjoy hearing the story, but my lips are sealed. This one's not coming from me—it's her life, and let me tell you, it's some mistake."

"Can I call her?"

He shook his head. "She's not at home. If you want to talk to Tamara, you'll have to go through my mom. Things have changed . . . a lot."

I took the bus home right after school and waited for Mom. As soon as she walked in the door, I begged her to call Mrs. Luchio. "Mom, you've got to help me. I have the feeling Tamara could be in more trouble now than when she was away. Jake talked like she was in prison or something."

"Leah . . . calm down." Mom thought about it. "I don't see any reason why I shouldn't call Bette Luchio."

"We have to make sure Tamara's okay."

I kept thinking of what Tamara had said before she left: "My mom really did do something terrible, and I'm the only one who knows."

I also remembered all the things Bette Luchio had found out from me, when the detective questioned me. Considering what I'd said about Tamara, Mrs. Luchio wasn't likely to feel kindly toward her daughter.

I watched Mom as she dialed the number. Then I listened.

"Hello, Bette? This is Jessica Lucas. . . . Yes . . . we're calling to see if Tamara's back—Leah was concerned. . . . It's been a week since the phone calls were located and she talked to Jake today. . . . No, he didn't tell her anything specifically. . . ."

There was a long silence on Mom's end as she listened to Bette Luchio talk. Mom's face grew red, and then she burst out in an angry tone. "None of this is Leah's fault, and I'm sorry you feel that way about my family and my friends. I work with kids every day, kids with parents like you."

Mom held the receiver away from her face. "She hung up on me."

I stood there, stunned, waiting for Mom to explain.

"I have to sit down after that phone call." Mom led the way into the kitchen.

"Mom, tell me!"

"You're going to be very upset, honey."

"Tell me!"

"She said they'd found Tamara mixed up with the wrong kind of people. Then she implied that Tamara had been under your influence and mine. She claimed that we had put certain ideas into Tamara's head."

"Mrs. Luchio said that?" I was shocked. "I've got to talk to Tamara!"

"She also said that Tamara was living someplace else, where she could make a new start, and that she no longer wanted you for a friend, and would you kindly stay away from their family."

"That's how she put it? That Tamara didn't want me for a friend?"

Mom nodded. "I'm sorry, Leah. I bet Tamara gets in touch with you and explains, but for now, your hands are tied."

Mom came over to hug me, and for the first time in months I put my head against her and cried. "It's not fair, Mom, it's just not fair."

"I know it, honey. I feel so sorry for Tamara."

127

But I was feeling sorrier for myself—I couldn't imagine not having Tamara for a friend! Even though I'd grown close to Miguel, I needed a girl to talk to and she was the only one who took my problems seriously, and at the same time, made me laugh.

When Miguel came over that week, we took long walks and talked. Even when I wasn't with him, I thought about him all the time. I could tell him everything, especially my feelings about Tamara, and he listened— sometimes just nodding, sometimes holding me.

Then Tuesday something strange happened. We were sitting on the couch, listening to Miguel's new tape, when the phone rang. I expected it to be Mom saying that she was held up at school.

"Hello?" I said. Then I heard it, the silence, just like before, the same muffled breathing. I'd never known that silence itself could have a pattern, distinct characteristics, but listening, I recognized that silence. "Tamara?"

I froze. She still wasn't talking! "I know you're back. Tell me where you are."

The line clicked dead.

"It must be Tamara," I told Miguel. "I mean, she stays on the phone until I start asking her questions, then she hangs up. I know she's trying to reach me. Only, this time I'm not telling anyone until she talks."

"What if she's in trouble with her mom?" He pulled me onto his lap and squeezed me around the waist.

"Then she'll have to let me know."

Just like before there was a pattern to the phone calls. A second call came at the same time, four o'clock, the very next day.

"Well, if she's not at her condominium, she must be someplace where she can call at that time. My guess is she's either at a school or a clinic of some sort," Miguel suggested.

"Yeah, but where?"

"She's probably at a private school . . . why don't we call Milwaukee Academy and see if she's enrolled there? That's about the only private school in this area—unless she's at a Catholic school."

Miguel pretended he was Leon Swiber, my counselor at Shorewood, and was calling to get the correct address so he could forward her records. After several practice attempts that ended in hysterical laughter, he dialed the number.

"Hello?" He spoke deeply. "My name is Leon Swiber, and I'm calling about a former student of mine, Tamara Luchio. I believe she's recently enrolled in your school, and I'd like to forward her records."

He paused, "Oh, I see, she started last Monday. Someone has already sent her records? Well, if there's anything else I can do to be of assistance, let me know. Thank you." As he hung up, Miguel burst out laughing again.

"But where is she living?" I asked.

He shook his head. "Look, at least you know she's still staying in touch, in spite of what her mother says. Right?"

"I guess."

He smiled and put his arms around me. "So when is your mom coming back?"

"Not until after the school board meeting."

Miguel whispered, "Alone at last." Then he closed the door to the hallway. "If your Mom or José come in early, they'll have to go through two sets of doors—we'll definitely hear them. I'll put on some music," he whispered.

As we lay on the rug, me propped up on an elbow,

129

Miguel flat on his back, I memorized everything about him, the mole near his right temple, the shape of his arm muscles, the softness behind each of his ears where there were still baby hairs. I even lifted his hands and massaged each finger, the hard calluses that came from plucking guitar strings. But more than anything else I liked his shape, the wideness across his shoulders, the way his hips narrowed, and the way his jeans hugged his seat. I fingered his chest, the hardness and smoothness of it.

"Do you wish I had hair there?" he asked, as I unbuttoned his shirt.

I smiled and kissed his chest. "I like it smooth."

"Can I unbutton your shirt?" he asked.

"Could we turn off the lights then?"

Miguel got up and flicked off the switch. Then we both sat on the floor in the dark while he unbuttoned my shirt. As he searched for the bra snap, his fingers tickled, which started me laughing.

"Hey, I never said I was an expert at this," Miguel whispered, giving up before he'd succeeded in undoing my bra. I felt relieved—it scared me to have him see me, the top of me, without clothes. It felt safer with my shirt and bra still on.

"Your fingers tickle." I giggled.

Gradually our eyes got used to the darkness. Lying next to Miguel, I felt his breath on my forehead. I could actually feel his heart beat when I lowered my ear to his chest.

"Leah?" He rolled to the side and propped himself on an elbow. "Is this okay with you?"

I smiled and kissed him, as we looked in each other's eyes for a few seconds without saying anything. "I like you." He grinned. "A lot."

"Me too."

"Are you sure?" he asked.

I hugged him, "Yeah, I'm sure."

We kissed then, a hard kiss, and he started wrestling, pinning me down. Then he leaned over and kissed me again, spreading his arms like a blanket over my arms. Suddenly he stopped and looked at me, his eyes wide. I could see drops of sweat on his face, his eyes softening. "How much do you like me?" he whispered. He hugged me close and rolled me over on top of him.

I pulled away and lay on my back. Neither of us spoke for a few minutes. We lay, side by side, listening to each other's breathing.

Finally I sat up. "Miguel?" I whispered.

He pulled me over so my head was on his chest, but the rest of me was lying next to him. We lay like that, warming each other. His fingers, the calluses, tickled the back of my shoulders under my shirt. It was so soft, so nice. I lay there, my head rising with each of his breaths.

Part of me wanted to cry, and part of me wanted to laugh—everything was moving so fast between us. All the touching had no place to go, but more of each other.

"I want you to love me before we go any farther," I whispered.

He didn't say anything, but his arms pulled me closer.

"I want our feelings to last."

Still, he said nothing. Only his hands moved up and down my back.

"I guess what I'm trying to say is that I want us to be in a real relationship. . . ."

I'd been holding back tears all evening, not sad tears, but tears from all the feelings inside. Somehow, when I admitted my feelings outright, the tears began to flow.

"Why are you crying?" Miguel asked.

131

"I don't know."

Miguel became quiet. I felt scared he might think I was trying to trap him, like Dad had always felt about Lucy. Yet he hugged me, gently.

"What do you think?" I finally asked.

"Let's get dressed and get something to drink."

I stared at him. "Are you mad at me for not doing anything?"

"No . . . not mad."

"Well, what then?"

"With you, it's probably better we wait."

What did he mean by that—with you. Would he do it with somebody else?

"It's okay like this," Miguel said. "Friendship first, right?"

Only, I didn't want to be friends first! I grabbed him and pulled him next to me on the couch. But just as I'd started to kiss him, Mom and José opened the sliding door. I guess my face was red from all the rubbing, and somehow we'd lost track of time. Anyway, we were on the couch, Miguel with his shirt off, in what Mom later claimed was a "dangerous position." The music was so loud, we hadn't heard them drive up.

Mom stopped, "Oh . . . ." She stood there, not knowing what else to say.

I'm not sure how much Mom and José knew before that evening, but afterward, they suspected too much.

José threw Miguel's shirt to him angrily. "Show some respect to Jessica. Put your shirt on. I think it's time for you to go home."

Miguel and I sat up quickly. When José told him to go, Miguel squeezed my hand hard, as if to say, *Don't worry,* and rose to leave without saying a word to José or Mom.

20

I took my cue and left José and Mom alone. It wasn't long before their voices rose in the kitchen, and even though Mom had shut the door, I could hear them from the bathroom.

"He's too old for her," Mom stated.

"I don't know about that . . . he's older, but only a year or so."

"Why would they get together when they both objected to our relationship in the beginning?" Mom asked. "Do you think they're getting back at us? Making us question our own relationship?"

José laughed. "I'm not sure why you're making such a big deal out of it, Jessica. They were just listening to music and kissing."

"Did you see her face?" Mom asked. "Did you notice her shirt wasn't tucked in? His shirt wasn't even on! He's a boy—you don't have to worry with boys."

"Wait a minute." José's voice grew angry. "No man in our family has ever shirked his responsibilities."

"Look, it's not just a coincidence that they've gotten involved—consciously or unconsciously, this has to do with us. It's some kind of rebellion. Against you and me."

"Both of them are lonely at their schools. . . ."

"How can you be so naive? Leah hated the idea of my dating you at the beginning, because"—Mom paused—"because you're Mexican! Now she's pretending to be in love with your nephew. Don't you find that strange?"

"What I find strange is your reaction." José's voice rose. "Why does there have to be a reason for two people to like each other? Why can't it just happen?"

"There doesn't have to be a reason for two people to like each other, but there does have to be a reason for two people to stay together."

"People create reasons to stay together," José stated angrily, "or they create reasons to drift apart."

"I just don't understand why he's not interested in an older girl."

"You really underestimate your daughter . . . just the way you underestimate yourself. Jessica, you can't fly off the handle each time Leah has a new boyfriend."

"Miguel seems so much older."

"Losing your parents makes you grow up fast."

"And Leah seems so young."

"I think you're reacting to our relationship—not theirs."

There was a long silence before Mom spoke. "You

134

should've found yourself a nice Catholic girl and pleased your mother."

"Come on, Jessica. Don't do that to me."

"If your mother finds out about Miguel and Leah, she'll put an end to it."

"I doubt Miguel and Leah are going to broadcast their relationship. My mother doesn't have to find out."

"It was rather obvious tonight."

"Look, Jessica. We're adults. I want to marry you. I want to have a family, and neither of us is getting younger. And in terms of Leah, I'm willing to take on the responsibility of your previous life. What more do you want? Why do you keep discussing us in terms of them? Let them lead their lives. Let us lead ours."

"I'm not sure I can separate my life from my daughter's."

"Well"—José's voice grew loud—"how long until you'll be sure? You're thirty-four. In two weeks you'll be thirty-five. I want to know then if you're going to marry me. I hate ultimatums, but I'm tired of all your fears keeping me at a distance. I want to plan a future with you." José paused. "And my family will accept whatever I choose."

"At my expense." Mom's voice was bitter. "How can you put a time frame on something like a marriage proposal? It's not fair."

"Nor is it fair to keep someone deeply in love . . . waiting."

I heard José walk out the back door, closing it quietly.

I was lying in bed when Mom knocked on my door.

"Leah? Can I come in?"

135

"Yeah."

"I want to talk to you."

"I've been expecting you," I told her.

"How much did you hear in the kitchen?"

"Everything."

Mom smiled, "And?"

"And I think you should marry him if you love him."

"I'm not referring to us. What about you and Miguel? You barely know him—and now you're practically molded to each other."

My face grew hot. "Mom . . . it's not like that. We were just listening to music."

Mom ran her finger up my chapped cheek. "That's not from cold weather."

"Okay. We like kissing. I'm fourteen, can't I have a boyfriend?"

"Is he your boyfriend?"

"Yes." I looked at my hands and avoided Mom's eyes.

"Can you tell me why you care about him so much when you objected to José?"

"They're two different people, Mom. Plus, I didn't really know any guys like them before."

"Like them?" Mom repeated sarcastically, rolling her eyes. "I'm glad it has only taken you four months to realize a human being is a human being. Sometimes I'm really scared by how narrow your life has been. You're so judgmental." Mom stared at me. "And anyone who doesn't fit the mold at your school has to prove himself."

"You're lecturing," I stated impatiently. "Anyway, I like Miguel and José now, so what's your point?"

"My point is they had to prove to you that they were worth liking! You judge people on the surface." Mom

136

pushed the hair off my face and whispered, "Do you think you're in love with him?"

"Mom, don't I have a right to keep some things private?"

"I'm asking because I want to know if I should be worried about you . . . you and him . . . you know?"

"No, you don't have to be worried about us. We're not going all the way."

Mom sighed deeply.

"Mom! I can't believe you're putting me through this."

"Only because I care," she whispered.

"Well, care a little less, then," I snapped back.

"Promise me something."

"What?"

"Be careful."

"Let's change the subject, Mom. What are you going to tell José?"

"Leah, do you know how hard it is to overcome such different backgrounds?"

"Meaning what, Mom? You just finished telling me we shouldn't judge people by their differences."

"Do you realize how all those things come out in a relationship? You've grown up without formal religion, without many people around, and you're used to a lot of space and privacy."

"So?"

"If you and Miguel were to get serious, you'd see that you'd be expected to go in the kitchen and talk with the women while dinner's being prepared, and you'd be expected to go to church Sundays, and you'd be expected to not work, to let the man support you, and you'd be expected to spend a lot of time with the relatives."

"Mom, we're not talking about Miguel and me, and if

137

we were, I wouldn't mind those things. Anyway, I don't think José expects any of that stuff from you."

Mom looked away.

"José's a great guy, Mom."

"I know," she whispered, "but for some reason that doesn't make it any easier."

21

hree days in a row the phone rang at four o'clock sharp. The chills I'd once gotten from the phone calls had worn off, and instead I felt a mixture of frustration and curiosity. Tamara had been found a week ago, and now we had two school days until vacation—I wondered, would she be home this Christmas?

I was already dreading the holidays. Miguel was scheduled to work full time. And José told Mom he wouldn't come over until she decided whether to marry him—he wanted to give her plenty of time to think things through, but Mom wasn't thinking, she was fuming, taking her loneliness out on me. Like yesterday afternoon.

When I got home, Mom was sitting at the kitchen table drinking a cup of coffee. She had on her favorite T-shirt that said, I PRAY TO GOD EVERY DAY, AND SHE ANSWERS MY PRAYERS.

I wondered if she was wearing that for José's sake—a challenge to his Catholicism or something.

"Where'd you get that?" Mom asked, pointing at my skirt. Her smile faded. "It's way too short. Looks cheap."

"I didn't ask you, Mom." I grabbed the pitcher of juice and poured a glass. "I saved the money from my birthday and bought some new clothes. I can pick out my own clothes with my own money, right?"

"Turn around," she said. "Where'd you get that sweater? I can see through it."

I could tell just by the way she sat up straight and her shoulders stiffened that she was about to criticize my sweater too.

"I thought you had plenty of clothes," Mom said.

"Miguel said I looked nice."

"No doubt."

"You don't have to make such a big deal out of one new outfit."

"You spend more time in front of the mirror these days than you do on your homework." Mom looked at her newspaper. "I can't keep track of all your clothes."

"Nobody's asking you to." I turned to go.

"Why do you have a scarf around your neck?" Mom teased. "Miguel isn't leaving any tracks, is he?"

I headed out the door, only as soon as I got outside, I realized it was almost four, and I'd have to answer the phone call from Tamara, so I headed back in, ignoring Mom's grin.

Only, that Thursday afternoon Tamara's phone call didn't come. All evening I worried. Then, the next morning, the day before Christmas vacation, something strange happened—I found a note left in my locker that said, *Meet me at Zack's, four o'clock, Christmas Eve.*

The only person who knew my locker combination was Tamara. As I read the note, my heart started pounding. Why was she being so secretive? Why had she chosen Zack's on Christmas Eve, a hamburger joint that had been closed down? Most of all, why had she left a note, instead of talking to me over the phone?

Then I remembered, we were invited to the Santiagos' Christmas Eve, at five o'clock, for an early dinner. I couldn't miss the dinner. Miguel had told me that his grandma has been cooking all week for us. But I had to see Tamara first, even if it meant being late to Mrs. Santiago's feast.

When Mom asked José over for dinner on Sunday night, I assumed that's when they were going to have their big marriage talk. It scared me that their relationship was uncertain—I wondered what would happen between Miguel and me if José ended up hating Mom for not marrying him. When I tried to talk to Mom about it, she just said, "I'm thinking about it." And Mom hadn't said anything about canceling out of Christmas Eve dinner at Mrs. Santiago's house, so I figured that maybe this Sunday, she and José wanted to spell things out before Christmas Eve arrived.

"I've asked José to bring Miguel for dinner too," Mom told me.

I'd been feeling really lonely because I hadn't seen Miguel in five days—he'd been working every day at Century Hall.

141

"José and I are going to a Christmas concert after dinner. Would you and Miguel mind cleaning up?"

"You're actually trusting us alone in this house?" I teased. "Aren't you afraid we'll lose control?"

Mom smiled. "Don't let me down."

"I promise nothing's going to happen."

It was the first holiday I'd ever celebrated with a real boyfriend. Sunday night I wanted to look special, so I pinned up my hair and wove a red velvet ribbon through the braid. I also put on a little mascara and eyeliner, along with some blush and eyebrow pencil. Lately Mom hadn't said anything about the small amounts of makeup I'd been wearing, so I figured she was lightening up on the issue.

Wrong assumption. As I was coming out of the bathroom, dressed in a black skirt and a white silk shirt, the doorbell rang. Mom beat me to it. I could tell she was happy to see José—she gave him a big hug. Miguel hugged me, too, right in front of Mom and José. And though I didn't care anymore, I couldn't help but notice his shiny, pointed-toe shoes—the kids at school called them sleaze shoes. But I kind of liked them on him, especially when he looked so handsome in his slacks and ironed shirt.

Suddenly Mom focused on me, heaving one of her loud, impatient sighs. "Miguel," she asked, "what do you think of girls who wear too much makeup?"

The room was silent. Miguel glanced at me, then shrugged.

"What do you think of Leah's new hairstyle, her new look!" Mom's voice was more of a statement than a question. José glared at Mom, and everyone stood there, embarrassed. "Leah's got this thing about makeup," she continued. "You're a man, Miguel, what do you think? Do girls look better or worse with all that junk on their faces?"

142

I was almost in tears.

Miguel's face turned red. "To tell you the truth, I can't really tell when she wears it. Does she have it on now?"

I almost died. I felt like a museum piece—everyone staring at my face, while Miguel talked. "If she has it on now, it looks good."

Mom rolled her eyes and looked at José. He grinned at me and raised his eyebrows at Mom. "I have to agree with Miguel. Leah looks beautiful tonight."

Mom shook her head. "All right. Overruled."

I couldn't believe it, Mom doesn't usually give up so easily. But then I heard Mom mumble just loud enough for everyone to hear, "Some women need a man's approval."

José came up and whispered, "You really look great! Don't worry, she's just being protective."

"Protective of what?" I whispered back. "I'm not her property."

"She's trying to protect your innocence." José grinned. "All mothers think that's their property."

I was relieved when dinner was over and Mom and José left. Miguel and I had a whole evening to ourselves. We made chocolate chip cookie dough and ate most of it before it got baked. And we lay on the couch, our bodies pressed together. I loved his skin, such smooth, hard muscles across his chest. I loved everything about him. "Have you missed me this week?" he whispered.

I smiled, nodding.

"Any chance they'll be home early?" Miguel asked, pulling me close.

"There's always a chance," I whispered. "Anyway, I promised she could trust us not to mess around."

"She can trust you, maybe . . ." Miguel laughed, turn-

143

ing off the light. "I never promised anything. . . ." He kissed me hard. "I missed you too."

"Miguel," I whispered as he hugged me tight, "I can't break a promise to Mom."

He kissed each of my eyelids, then my nose, then my lips. "I'm not asking you to."

Later, when I went to bed that night, I was surprised to find a small gift-wrapped box on my pillow. I knew right away it was my Christmas present from Miguel. He'd put it there when he went to the bathroom. I knew I should put it under the tree, but I couldn't wait three days, so I opened it. Inside was a lovely locket in the shape of a guitar, and a small gold necklace attached. Underneath was a note:

For Leah, he had written, *Love, Miguel.*

He'd signed it *love!* The word soared inside me—love! I barely slept that night, my body was so wide awake. For the first time I felt certain of his feelings.

Monday morning I went over to the South Side, to a record store that carried Latin music. I'd asked José what to get for Miguel, and he'd given me a list of records that he knew Miguel wanted.

As I got off the bus on the other side of the bridge, I felt I'd entered a different country. The restaurants had Spanish names and the stores had signs that said SE HABLA ESPA-ÑOL. Even the sign outside the huge stone church listed the services in Spanish. I felt like a foreigner. As I reached the record store, I hesitated. I wondered if the man inside the window spoke English. He saw me and nodded, so I finally got the nerve to walk inside.

"Excuse me, do you have any of these albums?" I handed him my list.

As he looked at the list, his eyes lit up, and he smiled broadly. "You like our music, yes?" In a very thick accent

144

he asked, "For you, these albums?" He waved the paper in the air.

"No, they're for my boyfriend. Do you have them?"

His smile fell, "You hear these music before?"

I shook my head.

He went to the back room and, returning, handed me four albums. "I give you a good price. Thirty-two dollars for all." He stared at me.

"Which two are the best?" I asked. "I can't buy them all."

His eyebrows narrowed as he stared out the window momentarily, then back at the albums. "These two, I like." He held up two, then set them down. "Maybe you like two others."

"I'll take the two you like," I said.

He wrapped them in tissue and put them in a bag. "Come back again."

The street was lined with stores and bars in a two-block radius—then, beyond, were old neighborhoods with large clapboard houses. Mrs. Santiago lived nearby, one bus stop over. As I passed the stores, I smelled something wonderful and looked up to see a bakery. I went inside and saw several women, speaking Spanish, sitting with coffee in front of them. There was laughter, voices rising and falling.

"Yes?" the woman behind the counter asked. I pointed to a roll, layers of crisp dough with guava filling inside. She put it in a bag for me, and as I walked toward the door, all the women nodded at me and smiled.

I suddenly realized, as I waited for the bus, that Miguel had spent most of his time here, in this world. I felt envious that his life contained such contrast. I'd never known neighborhoods like this existed right in the middle of Milwaukee.

In New York, yes, or Los Angeles, but I'd lived in Milwaukee for years, and I'd never seen this part of the South Side. I felt a certain sadness, that Miguel had shared my world with me, but until now, I'd never shared his.

22

I woke up early Christmas Eve morning and realized that in a few hours I'd see Tamara. José came over and told me not to eat any breakfast. "You'll be eating for three hours straight, once we get to Mom's house. She's the greatest cook in the world."

Mom looked up from her coffee and rolled her eyes. "Sounds Oedipal to me. What do you think, Leah?"

I wasn't quite sure what *Oedipal* meant, but I knew Mom was teasing, which was a good sign—it had been several days since Mom had joked around. Judging by her humor I guessed that maybe they were going to make some kind of announcement about wedding plans at Mrs. Santiago's dinner.

I didn't mention to José or Mom that I was meeting

147

Tamara. I told them I had last-minute Christmas shopping and that I'd meet them at Mrs. Santiago's house.

"Take the L bus, it brings you within a block," José said, "and it's direct from downtown."

"Great." Only, I wasn't really coming from downtown. I'd have to use my allowance and take a taxi. I told Miguel what was going on, just in case something happened. "I should be there on time, but if I get held up, don't let anyone get worried. I've got to go see Tamara, just to make sure she's not in trouble."

"Yeah. But try not to be too late. Grandma's worked all week on this dinner. It's a big deal to her."

As I took the bus to meet Tamara, I realized that even though I'd missed her a lot, I was scared to see her again. I'd waited so long to talk to her that I no longer knew what to expect. My feelings kept shifting. Sometimes I felt excited, and sometimes I dreaded seeing her because part of me suspected it would never be the same. And I hadn't forgotten our last conversation at the drugstore.

When I was about a block away, I saw a woman, but I didn't think it was Tamara. The person standing next to the pay phone had on gray slacks, a white scarf, and a blue coat. Her hair was longer than Tamara's, and smoothed back under a white beret. Suddenly, as I walked closer, I realized the person standing in front of me was no longer a flashy, weird dresser, but a younger version of Bette. Tamara stood before me without makeup and without her odd clothes. Tall, beautiful Tamara looked even taller and more beautiful.

She waved at me before I reached her, and if I hadn't been expecting her, I doubt I would have known who she

148

was. We hugged, and then Tamara quickly led me around back where the old picnic tables stood covered with snow. "Is this okay?" she asked, scraping off the bench.

"Sure," I said, "but why here? And why haven't you talked on the phone?"

Tamara sat down and began fiddling with her mittens. "I needed a chance to explain privately . . . and Glenview doesn't allow visitors. I'm not supposed to see you. I'm not supposed to hang around old friends."

"What's Glenview? Does Bette know you're seeing me?"

Tamara shook her head. "Bette's worse than ever. She thinks if she buys me a new wardrobe and sends me to a new school, I'll mutate into a decent person. I have to go along with whatever she says or else she'll send me to a boarding school. That's how pissed she is, just because she spent a ton of money finding me."

"Where did you go all that time?"

"You really aren't mad at me?" Tamara squinted in my direction and took a deep breath. "Still friends?"

"Yeah!"

"But I lied, about almost everything."

I heard the word *almost* louder than the rest.

"Bette, Dad, other men. I made it up, sort of, except that I kind of believed it myself after a while."

Suddenly I felt shy around Tamara.

She must have seen me glance at my watch, because she stood up. "Am I keeping you?"

"No, it's just that I'm supposed to go to this dinner, and I only have about fifteen minutes before I have to leave. I wish I didn't have to go, but I think Mom and José are going to make some kind of momentous announcement." I

149

looked at Tamara, hesitating, before I asked her, "So . . . what was it like in California?"

Tamara sat down again, sighing deeply. "I went to find my father, and I found him, all right." There was a long silence before she whispered, "He likes men."

I just nodded. Tamara looked up and stated, "Didn't you hear me? He likes men better than women, get it?" She had taken off her mittens and was rubbing her hands together before putting them back on.

At first I hadn't gotten it, but when she finished speaking, it sunk in.

"So how's your dad?" Tamara started talking fast, as though she needed to change the subject. "I wish we could go out and take some ski lessons. Is Prince Charming coming out here?"

"Tamara," I whispered, "was your dad nice to you?"

"Nice?" She laughed. "He's very nice, exceedingly nice." Then she looked away. "I guess I suspected it. At first, things were okay. He took me out to dinner, but it was hard to call him 'Dad,' so I called him Fred. Then, on the second day, he gave me money to get a plane ticket home. He told me he didn't want Mom to think he'd encouraged me to run away, and he was going to call her and tell her he was sending me home. He told me he thought about me and Jake a lot, but he didn't know how to be a father and he was too old to learn. The guy who lives with him, Sebastian, was really nice. Fred tried, but he just couldn't relate to me. It was like"—Tamara paused—"I don't know, like when we talked, our words never matched our feelings, like we said what we thought we should say, not what we felt, you know?"

"Are you glad you went?"

"I'm glad I saw him after such a long time. But it hurt

150

me when he handed me the money to fly home. I was sitting in his kitchen with a glass of juice, and he came down in his track suit and handed me an envelope. 'This is for your plane ticket home. I've made a reservation, and Sebastian will drive you to the airport.' That's all he said. Later, when I went into his study to tell him I was leaving, he turned and smiled, I guess he was relieved, and said, 'I'll phone your mother.' The way he said 'your mother' it was like he'd never met her before. Then, very politely he added, 'Thank you for coming. It was very nice to see you,' like I was some stupid guest. He gave me a hug, but only our arms touched, like he was afraid of me or something. I asked him if he could take me to the airport instead of Sebastian, but he said he had to work on the set."

"So, why didn't you come home then?" I asked.

"Because I didn't know what I'd tell everyone here." Tamara leaned back and took a deep breath. "Promise not to hate me?"

I nodded.

"After Sebastian dropped me off at the airport, I took a bus to the boardwalk where I met this guy named Rich. He asked me to a party. We ended up getting high . . . and I stayed with him." Tamara looked at me. "I mean, I stayed with him for a couple of days."

"Where'd you meet him?" I asked. "How old was he?"

"He was nineteen. I met him in this comic-book store where he works." Tamara braided the threads at the end of her scarf as she talked, "I should have left while I had the money. But Rich kept spending it, and I felt older, freer, you know? At first I told him I was older, but a few days after we met, I told him the truth and he freaked. We went to his friend's house for a party, and he left me there. Talk about being depressed. There were a couple of other girls

151

who lived there. One of them told me I should call home and get someone to come get me. She had men's names tattooed on her shoulders. Listening to her talk about guys, I got scared, so I started calling you, only I was afraid to talk, afraid you'd tell everyone, and then they'd find me there, and I didn't know what Bette would do."

Tamara was getting tears in her eyes. "I used Dad's money for food, and I stayed in that house because there was no place else to go. At least Denise was nice—she's the girl with the tattoos. And I kept calling you just to keep in touch with someone. It was like another world there."

Tamara looked away. "That's when I sent you and Bette the postcards. Bette had already been in touch with Dad, and she'd hired a private detective to find me. I didn't realize until later that they found me because they'd traced the phone calls from your house."

For a moment I felt jealous of Tamara. Her life made mine seem boring. And looking at her now, thin and tan and mature, I wondered if we would still be close or would my life sound dumb to her? I touched Tamara's shoulder. "So, is it good to be home?"

"I've only been home for a day. That's how come I couldn't see you. I've been at Glenview, this stupid halfway house for runaways—part of my agreement with Bette. It's Bette's version of blackmail."

"Why?"

"Bette's totally freaked out about this—she's like obsessed with what people will say about her—Mother of the Runaway Daughter!" For the first time Tamara started laughing. "I had a choice, either Glenview or a girls' boarding school. Big choice—Glenview's eight weeks, boarding school's for three years. I've only had to live at Glenview for the first two weeks, and from now on I just go there after school for the group sessions, but I get to go home at night."

"But why didn't you talk to me before? Why the silent phone calls?"

"I told you already. I'm not allowed to contact old friends. I'm not supposed to even see you because the counselors say the old friends are part of the problem." Tamara smiled at me. "That's why I had to see you in secret." Tamara's eyes grew wide. "See, Bette said that if I don't shape up—that's her term—I'm going to have to go to this snobby girls' school in Virginia where you have to wear uniforms and study all the time."

"She's serious about sending you away?"

"Mmm-hmm. She had the brochures lying on the dining room table. So I had to promise to go to Milwaukee Academy, which is almost as bad. All the little rich snobs talk about is their stupid PSAT scores and their SAT scores and whether they'll apply to Stanford or Smith. And Bette thinks it's a better environment for me, but she only thinks that because she sees all the parents drive up in Mercedeses to drop their kids off."

"When did you leave the note?"

"I had to get to Shorewood by seven on Friday morning."

"Does Jake know everything?" I asked. I was worried he might tell Rachel, and then everyone would find out. "He and Rachel are friends, you know."

Tamara nodded. "He knows some of it, like about Dad. But he doesn't know the details about Rich. Anyway, Jake went out with Rachel only once. He said she spent the whole time pumping him for information about me. And you."

153

"Well, there's one thing Rachel doesn't know about me." I smiled. "I've got a boyfriend now."

Tamara rolled her eyes, "My condolences. Believe me, they're not worth the trouble. I know!"

"Miguel's different," I stated. "He really is."

"That's what *I* thought." Tamara laughed bitterly. "I thought Rich was different when I met him. Look where it got me—Glenview!"

There was a long silence between us. I took a deep breath, trying to cool off my anger. "Miguel is different."

"Mind if I ask how long it's been going on?"

"Long enough," I said, pausing. "Long enough."

"And how long is long enough?" Tamara laughed. "I've only been gone five weeks, and you didn't have a boyfriend when I left."

"Look, Tamara"—I stared right at her—"he's a good friend, he's honest!"

She took off her mittens and began to pick at her thumbnail. Without looking at me she whispered, "Sorry."

"I'm sorry too. I didn't mean to say that about honesty."

"Where did you meet him?"

"He's José's nephew." I was just about to say she should meet him, but I stopped myself—Tamara was beautiful now, and Miguel might like her looks better than mine.

"Do you see him a lot?"

"I talk to him every day."

"Oh, great." She laughed sarcastically. "You're the only person I came home to see, and now you won't have any time left over for me!"

"Tamara, that's stupid." But even as I spoke, I knew it wouldn't be the same as before she'd left, when all my free time had been spent with her.

154

"Have you told him our secrets?"

"No." Which wasn't completely true—I'd told him some of them.

She stared at me. "Are you closer to him than me?"

"Tamara, that's really a dumb question."

She looked away and laughed as she spoke. "I don't want stuff I tell you to go to him, and if you're closer to him . . ."

"It's different with a guy, you know? It's a different kind of closeness."

"Very diplomatic, Leah." She squinted at me. "How is it different?"

I laughed. "Three-alarm chili."

"Obviously, it's different in that way." Her voice wavered. "You're not going to be like Bette, are you? When she gets a new boyfriend, he replaces everyone else in her life. And she always says the same thing that you're saying—it's a different kind of closeness she has with her boyfriends than with me."

"But it is different with a guy!"

"Yeah, well, it seems like that kind of closeness always takes priority." Tamara looked away.

"Tamara, he's my boyfriend and you're my best friend. Anyway, he goes to a different school!"

"Well, so do I now!" she said sadly. "And Bette's going to make it hard for us to spend time together—it's got to be a secret."

I walked Tamara toward the bus stop, but when a car drove by, she turned quickly to hide her face. "You never know who's going to see us."

"Bette would really send you away?" I asked.

"She'd love an excuse—I've never seen her this angry."

As we hugged, Tamara whispered, "Remember, don't call me."

155

23

"Where have you been all this time?" Miguel whispered as he answered the door. "This isn't the best way to make a good impression!"

Everyone was silent when I entered the room. "I took the wrong bus. I'm sorry."

José glared at Mom, then me. "Forgot to take the L, huh?"

Mrs. Santiago served sherry on a tray with little mushrooms stuffed with crabmeat. Then we sat down and ate salad first, followed by soup, then the main course, which was roast beef and potatoes au gratin. The reason I mention the food first is because that was the best part of the whole day, and if we had all just kept eating, the evening might have gone okay, but everyone seemed tense, right from the

156

beginning. At first I thought it was because I'd come late, but then, when the silences grew longer, I thought it had to be something else. I mean, silence is a miracle when Mom and José are in the same room.

What bothered me most was that from the moment I arrived, Miguel acted strange. He barely smiled at me, and he didn't touch me or hold my hand. After the first five minutes he stopped looking at me altogether. I tried to catch his eyes, but he just stared at whoever was talking, usually José or Mrs. Santiago.

Actually, I felt angry. Not that I wanted him to kiss me or anything, but there are small ways to show we like each other, without being obvious.

My stomach felt full even before we sat down at the table. Throughout the meal I could hear the forks and knives tinkling against the plates. It seemed embarrassing that all of us could sit there and eat without saying anything to each other. Like we were waiting for something to happen . . .

José tried to start up a conversation by complimenting his mother. "Now I know why I've never been skinny. I can't refuse the world's best cooking." And his mother's little head nodded as she explained how she prepared each course. The more I looked at her, the more beautiful I thought she was, like Miguel, with carved, straight features and deep, dark eyes. On her wrists were beautifully decorated bracelets, and when the room became really quiet, we could hear them jingle, almost as if they were trying to stir up our conversation.

I guess I should have noticed sooner, but I didn't, not until after the main course. Mom asked Marisol, that's Mrs. Santiago's first name, how she found time to do everything

157

—garden, cook, tutor children in Spanish. "You're amazing," Mom said stiffly. "There's nothing you can't do!"

I thought Mom was being nice, but then I saw José's face turn red, his eyes glaring in Mom's direction. Plus, there was a long silence after Mom paid Mrs. Santiago the compliment, and Mrs. Santiago stopped smiling for about thirty seconds as she excused herself to get dessert. Then Miguel excused himself and said he had to get a pitcher of water. I guess I must have been blind, because suddenly it was quite apparent that there was a fight going on—between Mom and José.

The silence seemed to go on forever, until Mrs. Santiago returned with the dessert. She looked at José. "I've made so much of everything. Perhaps you can take some home and freeze it. That should ease the strain on Jessica when she goes back to work."

Mom didn't answer, she just looked at José, who spoke up. "Thanks, Mom, we'd love to take home the leftovers."

"After all, you're about to marry one," Mom whispered sarcastically, loud enough so everyone could hear.

Suddenly José's fist hit the table. "Why? Why do you have to do this now?"

"Because they're doing it, you're just too blind to see it. They always talk to you, instead of me, as if I'm somehow infected with a contagious disease."

"That's in your head!" José yelled. We all sat still. "You need your head checked! You think everyone is out to exploit you . . . or your daughter! Why don't you grow up and stop trying to make everyone else pay for your past?"

Mom stood up, her face enraged. "No! You need to untie your mother's apron strings—no one can live up to her. No one. I'm sick of the way your family talks as if I'm not really here. They always make me feel like an outsider.

158

First there was the issue of my divorce. Then the fact that because I'm a mother—God forbid I should work full time and go to school. Forgive me for wanting a career!" Mom let out a queer laugh and wiped her eyes. "Then there are the constant comparisons they make, between my life and your sister's life. You don't even realize how often you compare me to your sister."

I looked up to see Miguel and Mrs. Santiago looking worried as they stood in the doorway.

"Maybe they're right," Mom cried. "Maybe you deserve someone better. But I'm sick of them handling me with rubber gloves, as if touching me might contaminate them. I'm sick of getting criticized because I want to be independent." Mom paused and took a deep breath, glaring at José. "Sure we'd love the leftovers. Isn't that why we were invited in the first place, to make sure you get at least one balanced meal? After all, your mother hasn't asked me one question since we got here."

"We're not talking about independence," José yelled back. "We're talking about selfishness. You're not afraid to lean on me, when you need me to fix the car or tighten the kitchen plumbing or shovel the walks. You just don't want anyone leaning on you—that's the problem."

José looked at me and nodded. "I'll take you both home now." His voice wasn't particularly nice to me either. Then I glanced at Miguel, but both he and his grandma had disappeared into the kitchen.

Just as we were about to walk out the door, Mrs. Santiago came into the hallway, followed by Miguel. "No, you cannot leave like this, please wait. For a minute, stay, let's talk."

We kept on our coats, but sat on the living room couch

159

—José, Mom, and me, facing Mrs. Santiago and Miguel as they sat in chairs across from us.

"You are right, I do not talk to you like my son. But not for those reasons. In my family the women talk separately. You are different from my generation, yes. And I do not like many of the changes, I admit. I do not know how to talk about your life, school, and work and such things. I have not done those things myself. And sometimes I wish for José a simpler life, perhaps a simpler woman. But I am not blind. I do know he loves you, and he has never loved a woman like this. I would like for him to have a child." She looked at me and smiled. "Another child." There was a pause and a long sigh. "I wish for both of you an easier time, not life like this, filled with fighting. And, yes, I would like for you to come visit more often and take home what I have to offer—not because I think you can't do it, too, but because it makes me feel needed. José is my oldest. You must know how that is." She looked at Mom, then me, and smiled wider. "The oldest is a child and a companion, yes?"

Mom smiled and stood up. "Yes," she answered, and walked over to hug Mrs. Santiago. I could see that both Mom and Mrs. Santiago had tears in their eyes. Finally Miguel smiled at me, but by that time, after he had ignored me all evening, I was too angry to care. Before he had a chance to say anything, Mom and José had loaded my arms with loaves of fresh bread, and we were piling into the car.

24

The plan was that after we left the Santiagos, we were going to go back to our place and decorate the tree. Then, about ten-thirty, José would leave for Mass. But in an effort to be nice to José and in order to prove she wasn't selfish, Mom offered to go along to Christmas Eve Mass. I decided not to go. I was too mad at Miguel to enjoy listening to him sing.

Mom described it to me later, how they sat in a pew near the front of the church. After a long wait the priest said a prayer in Spanish and the choir came in wearing robes and carrying candles—first the women, then the men. They could hear the soprano, alto, tenor, bass voices pass by in order, each pair of faces lit by candles.

"He looked like an angel," Mom told me. "When his

161

solo came, we were all wiping our eyes. His voice echoed through the entire chapel."

While they were at church, Dad called exactly at midnight. "I wanted to be the first to wish you a Merry Christmas."

"Thanks, Dad."

"For your Christmas present—"

Which he hadn't sent, I thought to myself.

"—I'm coming to visit your Grandma Lucas in January, and as a present, I want you to come, with a friend, and spend a weekend with me in Chicago at a hotel. There's a pool and floor show, and we can take in a play or something, okay? So you invite someone."

"Can I invite a guy?"

"Who?"

"My boyfriend."

"You have a boyfriend?" Dad asked. "Does your mother approve?"

"She introduced us."

There was a long pause, then Dad cleared his voice. "He's not one of her problem students, is he?"

"No, he's . . ." I paused. I was just about to say he was José's nephew when I realized that Dad might automatically dislike him if he knew that. "He's a great guy, Dad."

"That would mean an extra room."

"You could share a room with him, and I'd share with Lucy."

"Don't you have a girlfriend you could bring?"

"Don't you want to meet my boyfriend?"

Dad laughed. "We'll talk more about it before you come. I miss you, honey."

"Me, too, Dad."

After he hung up, I wondered what Dad would say

when he found out Miguel was Mexican. For the first time I understood how sad Mom must have felt before, when I had made fun of José.

I woke early Christmas Day, partly because I expected Miguel to call. I hadn't had a chance to give him my present—all day I waited.

When the phone rang around eight in the evening, I thought for sure it would be him and was surprised to hear Tamara's voice. "Merry Christmas," she whispered. "What did Santa bring you?"

"A sweater and some earrings. Mom's going to let me pierce my ears, finally."

"Lucky."

"And Dad called and asked me to meet him in Chicago for a weekend."

"Oh, great, I can take the bus down and meet him." Tamara suggested.

I realized I shouldn't have mentioned the trip—I wanted to ask Miguel, not her.

"When is he coming? I'll have to plan it so Bette doesn't know."

"I don't know. It's not even for sure yet," I said, "and you never know with Dad, anyway." Then, changing the subject, I asked, "What did Santa bring you?"

"New clothes. I feel like Bette's Barbie doll."

"Miguel gave me perfume."

"Nice." She paused, then whispered, "I'm bored . . . holidays are so dull around here. Bette hasn't stopped smiling all day."

"Is Leonard spending Christmas with you?"

163

Suddenly the phone went dead, and a few minutes later, when it rang again, I ran to answer it.

"Is your mother there, Leah?" It was Mrs. Luchio.

I ran and got Mom, who began shaking her head when I told her who was on the phone. "Not now, it's Christmas. She's not going to ruin a nice day, is she?"

Mom's voice sounded strained. "Hello, Bette." She listened for what seemed like a long time, then spoke loudly.

"I can't control their phone calls. . . . No, I won't insist Leah hang up on her. Thank you for calling." Mom slammed the phone down on the receiver.

A half hour later the doorbell rang. It was nine o'clock, so this time I was positive it would be Miguel. But it was Tamara! She'd taken a cab from her mom's house.

As soon as I opened the door, she burst out crying. "Bette says she's sending me away after Christmas break, just because I called you."

As I made introductions, Tamara stared at Mom and José, then at our house. Suddenly I realized it was the first time she'd ever been over. Mom and José told her to come into the living room and sit down, and José poured her some wassail.

"Leonard's left and she blames me. God, she treats Jake so different from me. She said it's my fault Leonard left. She blames me for all the men leaving, but it's not like that. She says Leonard couldn't stand me, and when I ran away, he realized that I was always going to be a problem for them. But the real problem is Bette. One minute she's nice, the next she's awful. Like today, she gave me all these nice clothes, and we went out to lunch to celebrate Christmas, and then, just because I called you, she freaks out and threatens to send me away."

164

"Tamara"—Mom spoke calmly—"does she know where you are right now?"

"No."

"Don't you think we should call her?"

"No! She just wants to send me away."

"Why is she so set on sending you away?" José asked.

"She says she can't control me—that I'm uncontrollable." Tamara's eyes scanned each of us and settled on me. "It's like I said before, Bette did something bad once. And she won't forgive me for finding out. She thinks I'm out to ruin her life or something."

We all listened. I only hoped she was telling the truth this time.

"Saul gave Bette these sleeping pills. This was when we were pretty young, like five and six. Anyway, Saul used to love to spend time with us, but Mom hated to have us around all the time because we always fussed and spied on them." Tamara paused. "It was Saul's birthday, and Mom put two of the sleeping pills in our juice so we'd fall asleep early. I saw her crush them, and when I asked her what the pills were, she told me vitamins. But after we'd gone to bed, Jake had an allergic reaction to the stuff. He broke out in hives, and his whole body started to itch. He gets asthma from allergies, too, and he couldn't breathe, so Saul had to rush him to the hospital. When he brought Jake home, he asked me if Jake had taken any medicine, and not realizing what I was doing, I showed him Bette's pills and told him she had put them in our dinner. Saul was so mad, he stopped seeing Bette, and about a week later he dropped dead. Now, every time a guy breaks up with Bette, she thinks it's something I've said or done."

"She's probably never forgiven herself," Mom whispered.

165

"Could you talk to her, Mrs. Lucas?" Tamara asked.

Mom shook her head. "It would probably make matters worse. You and Leah are too close for me to get involved."

"I'll talk to your mother," José said. "It might not do any good, but I'll try. We had a good talk at the Thanksgiving party."

Tamara's face relaxed. "Really? You'll talk to her even though you barely know me? She'll listen to you—you're a vice-principal. And she listens to men."

José smiled. "I'll drop by your place tomorrow."

Mom offered to drive Tamara home, and by the time she left, it was already nine-thirty—all I could think about was Miguel . . . where was he? Why hadn't he called or come over?

José saw me remove the gifts I'd gotten Miguel from under the tree. "Miguel was pretty upset after dinner the other night—the fight at Mom's house—I don't think he's coming tonight, Leah."

"But why's he upset with me?"

"I think it might have to do with your not coming to Mass with us, but you'll have to ask him." José put his arm around my shoulder. "I'm sure it'll pass."

"Here," I said, almost in tears. "Give him these presents, okay?"

I lay awake a long time that night, still hoping, somehow, Miguel would come over. But he didn't, and the next morning I woke up sad, feeling that things might have changed without my knowing it.

The day after Christmas I stayed home, waiting for a phone call. It was almost noon when the phone finally rang.

"God, José's something else," Tamara said as soon as I picked up the receiver. "He actually talked Bette into a great compromise. Bette really liked José. It's the first com-

166

promise she's ever made in her entire life. I dress her way, keep up my grades, go to summer school to make up for last semester, stay home weeknights, plus see a counselor with her, and I not only get to stay, but I also get to come back to Shorewood. Great, huh?"

"Great," I said.

"You don't sound too thrilled."

"I am, it's just that I need your advice."

"You're asking me for advice?"

"I don't know what to do," I explained word for word the evening at Miguel's grandma's. "He hasn't been in touch in forty-eight hours. Mom and José went to Mass, but I was too angry, and I think he might be mad that I didn't go hear him sing."

"Well, you've got me to talk to—now that Bette's lifted my ban on phone calls." Tamara sounded almost happy that Miguel and I hadn't spoken in two days. "I may not be three-alarm chili, but . . ."

"Thanks for the great advice, Tamara."

She paused. "Well, I think I'd call him if I were you."

"Me call him?"

"Why not? Ask him why the sudden change?"

"But then he'll know how much I need him!"

"So what?" She gave a loud sigh. "Maybe he should know."

"But we haven't known each other that long," I admitted. "He'll think I'm weird if he finds out how I feel."

"Look, up until now he's done all the calling, right?"

"Right."

"Don't be a Rachel Spencer—she thinks you have to win guys like they're trophies. Jake told me he can't stand the way Rachel's always trying to outdo everyone, even him."

167

"What else did he tell you?"

"Don't change the subject." Tamara laughed. "What good is a relationship if you can't be honest with each other?"

"Tamara," I asked, "were you honest with the guy in California?"

Tamara paused. "Leah, can I ask you a personal question?" She hesitated. "A chili-soup kind of question?"

"I haven't done it yet, if that's what you're wondering."

"No . . . but does it matter"—Tamara's voice cracked —"that I have?"

At first I was stunned. Hearing her admit it out loud—I didn't know what to say. "No, I guess not. I mean, I knew you had because of the way you talked about California." I hesitated. "Did you love him?"

She took a deep breath. "I thought so, but now I realize I was just trying to make him love me."

"Was it okay?" I stammered. "I mean, was it fun?"

"No." Tamara sighed. "I was high a lot, so I don't even remember that much."

"I'm glad you're home," I whispered.

"Call him and talk to him," Tamara stated. "Don't waste a whole week worrying about him. And if he's nice, he'll be glad you called to talk it out."

"You really think so?"

"Call me afterward."

"It's okay with your mom if I call?"

"Yep. It's part of our new deal—thanks to José."

Knowing I could talk to Tamara later gave me the courage to call Miguel.

But as I dialed the number, my hand was shaking.

"Hello?" It was Mrs. Santiago!

168

"Is Miguel there?" I asked in a whisper. I didn't want her to recognize my voice.

"He's working. Who's calling please?"

"A friend from school. Thanks," I said, hanging up.

"Mom, I'll be home before dark," I yelled. "I'm going for a walk."

"No later!"

25

I took the bus, which has a direct line right down the street where Miguel works, but when I got to Century Hall, I suddenly panicked—what if the building was locked?

Which it was, at least from the front. So I went around back and knocked on the back door. When no one answered, I tried to open it, and much to my surprise it was unlocked.

There was Miguel, a white apron wrapped around his body, stacking dishes.

He looked up, stunned. "What are you doing here?" he asked, his eyes wide. "How'd you get in? How'd you know where I was?"

"I've got to talk to you," I stated.

"I know." Miguel's face broke into a smile. "I'm almost done. Better wait outside for me, so Sheila doesn't get pissed. We're not supposed to let people into the kitchen." He walked me over to the door. "I'll be out soon, and we can head back toward your house."

Even though it was freezing, I didn't mind waiting. The snow had started falling in huge, wet flakes by the time Miguel joined me. "I'm glad you came." He hugged me. "I love the albums. Thanks."

"Why didn't you come over Christmas night, like we'd planned?"

"Why didn't you come to Mass with your Mom and José?" Miguel looked away. "At the dinner I guess I was angry . . . at your mom. It was like she didn't try to understand the differences between our family and yours. It made me think about things . . . between us."

"But you were really cold to me, even before their fight."

Miguel's arms circled my waist, and his mouth was pressing down on mine. It felt so good.

He pulled me over to the bench on the edge of the park and we sat down. His fingers were at the nape of my neck, tugging my hat, combing through my hair. "See, your mom's partly right. Grandma does prefer Mexican girls, but only because she understands them." Miguel smiled. "See, if I show I like you, more than just as a friend, Grandma wouldn't approve. Grandma's got plans for me—she's always telling me I'm the one to carry on the traditions because of my music."

"If she doesn't like me, will that change how you feel?"

He raised his eyebrows and smiled. "It's not like she has to know." Miguel leaned over to kiss me, but I backed away.

171

"But why didn't you come over Christmas night?"

Miguel shrugged. "I guess I just needed some space. The argument between your mom and José really got to me. And I guess I was angry you didn't come to hear me sing." He gave my hand another squeeze. "It just seemed like suddenly everything was getting complicated. I like things simple between friends, you know?" Miguel pulled me close.

"But I like you more than just as a friend," I whispered.

"But it's not like we're ready to get married and settle down." He laughed. He massaged the back of my head as he kissed me.

Only, what he'd just said bothered me.

"Miguel?" I stopped kissing and sat back. I wanted to ask him what he meant when he said he liked to keep things simple and he wasn't ready to settle down—did that mean he didn't want a girlfriend? Wasn't I his girlfriend?

"Yeah?" He smiled at me.

But I was too scared to ask, too scared to hear his answer.

"Nothing," I whispered.

He pulled me close again, and we sat for a few minutes, watching the snow fall. Then I felt it—his hand slowly moving underneath my coat, from my back, around my waist, then up my front, underneath my shirt and bra.

"Okay?" he whispered.

But it was almost dark and I needed to get to the nearest bus stop, so I took his arm and pulled him up from the bench. "Mom will kill me if I'm not home by dark."

"Couldn't you tell her the bus got a flat tire?" he asked hopelessly.

*　　*　　*

172

"What happened?" Tamara asked, as soon as I called her.

"Chili to the max," I whispered, "and the second baseman made a catch."

"Did he steal the base or was it a fly ball?" Tamara let out an uncontrollable burst of laughter.

"Second baseman lost the ball." I giggled.

Tamara paused. "So, are you glad you called him?"

"Yeah, really glad. But it's still hard for me to tell him exactly how I feel. The words just don't come out when I'm with him."

"Everyone feels that way."

"Are you ready for school?" I asked.

"No. Jake said people called me 'fried chicken' before because my hair looked fried."

That was true, but I didn't want to rub it in. "Don't worry about it. I'll meet you before school."

26

Tamara really did look different in a way that made me not want to stand too close to her at school. I didn't want anyone to compare us. She had on a pink-and-white tweed shirt, a matching white sweater, and nylons with leather shoes. She looked better than most college students. Her hair was smoothed back, away from her face, so her eyes, without any makeup, looked darker than I had remembered. She really was beautiful, probably more beautiful than any other girl at our school. And even though she was my best friend, I have to admit, it was a little difficult to take the big change in her looks, especially because Bette went out and bought Tamara a whole new wardrobe and paid to have Tamara's hair styled. Tamara didn't brag about her new clothes, but I could tell just from looking at

174

her that her mom had spent a lot of money. I also knew there was no way Mom could afford to do stuff like that for me, so I tried not to think about Tamara's and my differences. But for once I was glad Miguel went to another school.

"Well, these lockers smell just the same." Tamara opened the metal door and waved her hand in front of her nose. "Smells like somebody dipped a jock's sock in milk and hung it up to dry." She giggled.

Just then, out of the corner of my eye, I noticed Rachel Spencer and her friend, Samantha, approaching. I elbowed Tamara to hurry, but she didn't catch on.

"Boy, have you changed!" Rachel said, as she spotted Tamara.

Tamara turned and smiled in her direction. "Hi, Rachel, hi, Samantha."

"So, what did you learn in California," Rachel asked, "that you couldn't have learned here?"

I wished Tamara would hurry. I wasn't in the mood for one of Rachel's attacks, especially with Samantha at her side. I had this feeling about Rachel: anywhere there were secrets, she would sniff them out. But Tamara insisted on taking her time, organizing her books and notebooks.

"So how was it?" Samantha repeated.

"You seem to have lost your tan!" Rachel added. "How long have you been back?"

Tamara turned and faced them. "You look wonderful, Rachel. So do you, Samantha." It was like putting up a white flag—surrender! Couldn't she see they were trying to put her down?

"I hear you're going to have to repeat a year," Rachel said, "unless you take summer school. Jake told me."

"Yeah, actually just one semester." Tamara nodded.

175

"Well, welcome back."

"Yeah," Samantha repeated. Then she and Rachel walked down the hallway as I stood staring in total disbelief. Why had Tamara been so friendly?

Tamara grinned. "I don't want to get all cliquey again. You know, them against us. Not that I want to be their best friend either."

"I don't act cliquey like them!" I stated. "I don't try to put people down like Rachel does. She always acts as if she's better than everyone else."

"You sometimes put her down. We both do."

I walked next to Tamara, without speaking, gripping my books like a shield. "Boy, you have changed!"

"Come on," Tamara said, still smiling. "We've both changed—about one hundred percent. I don't want to go back to how I was, do you?"

Part of me did want to go back, I realized. Part of me wished life could be as simple as it was before this year. But then I thought about Miguel—I wouldn't know him then!

"You're not half as shy as you used to be," Tamara added. "I mean, you called Miguel up, and you went over and found him at work. That takes guts!"

The more Tamara talked, the better I felt. Only, the bell rang, so we couldn't talk anymore, not until lunchtime, when we took our bag lunches and sat outside the auditorium where we could be alone.

"Who do you have in your classes?" I asked, referring to the guys.

"Well," Tamara whispered, "Caesar's in my English class."

"Do you still like him?"

Tamara twisted her face. "I like his body. But he can barely read. He couldn't even fake answers in class. All he

176

did was stare at the book when the teacher called on him. Talk about embarrassing."

"Did he notice you were back?"

Tamara rolled her eyes. "Unfortunately. He actually walked me down the hallway."

"Who else is in your classes?" I guess I was hoping that Tamara would fall for someone fast, so I wouldn't have to worry about Miguel going for her.

"No one worth dying over." Tamara grinned. "We should clone your Dad—when's he coming, anyway? Meeting him is like the only thing I have to look forward to." She looked up and must have seen me looking worried, because she added quickly, "And meeting Miguel, of course. I'm looking forward to that. The guys here are pitiful."

"Yeah." I smiled. "Nothing much changed while you were away." Except I knew Tamara was going to be popular with the guys in a way she hadn't been before.

"Hey, wait up!" Even before I turned to look, I recognized the voice. Rachel and Samantha were hurrying to catch up with us as we headed for the bus stop. "We want to hear more about California. Why'd you end up coming back, anyway?" Rachel asked breathlessly, as she approached us.

Tamara glanced at me and shrugged. "It wasn't what I thought it'd be," she said. "I missed things here."

"Like Caesar? I saw you walking down the hallway with him today." Rachel raised her eyebrows. "Did he ask you out?"

"No way!" Tamara giggled.

Rachel looked disappointed. "Well, anyway, Samantha

177

and I are planning a party—it's Samantha's birthday. She's turning fifteen. We called Jake last week," Rachel continued, "and he told us you were back. Anyway, when we asked to talk to you, he said you're at another number, but he wouldn't tell us why."

What nerve they had!

Tamara was staring at the kids passing us, heading for the bus.

"Don't you live with your mother anymore?" Rachel asked.

Tamara nodded, but the nerve under her right eye was twitching. "I'm home now. I was just visiting some friends someplace else."

"Where?" Rachel asked, suddenly excited.

"What kind of place?" Samantha repeated.

I was just about to scream at them to stop, when Tamara turned and looked Rachel right in the eye. "None of your business." Tamara smiled. "I wouldn't be able to come to your party anyway, the next three weeks are tied up with homework. But you can reach me at my mom's anytime. Jake said you had lots of questions about me and Leah, so now you can call and ask me personally."

Rachel and Samantha just stood there, trying to cement smiles on their faces. I grabbed my stuff and followed Tamara. So, she hadn't changed totally, I thought happily.

27

Yesterday I got the money for two train tickets, along with a note from Dad:

Bring a guest—male or female—the four of us will have a great time. Take a cab to the Radisson, downtown. (Enclosed is a check to cover the fare.) We'll be waiting. Love, Dad.

I told Mom and she immediately saw my problem. "Who are you going to invite, Miguel or Tamara?"

"I want to invite Miguel, but then Tamara will be really hurt. I promised her a long time ago that she'd get to meet Dad. She's been obsessed with him ever since I told her he was head of a ski school." I stood next to Mom and watched her stir-frying vegetables. "How do you think

179

Dad's going to react when he finds out Miguel's related to José?"

Mom laughed. "I'd invite Tamara if I were you."

"Yeah, but she'll flirt with Dad and make Lucy mad."

Mom tasted a mushroom. "So, go by yourself."

"But I want Miguel to meet Dad."

Mom turned to me, her expression serious. "Miguel would probably be relieved not to be invited. Most boys don't want to meet their girlfriend's fathers."

"Most fathers are not as funny as Dad."

"What if Miguel doesn't want to go?"

I stared at her. Truth was, I couldn't imagine spending a weekend away from him, especially now that he was working so much. We only got to see each other after school one day a week, and the only time we could really be together, alone together, was weekends. I thought of how much I missed kissing him on the days I didn't see him—no way could I go without seeing him for a whole weekend.

Mom sat down next to me. "Why don't you ask Tamara —you don't spend nearly as much time together now as you did before."

"Two months ago you didn't want me to spend so much time with her," I replied angrily.

"Leah, if you promised Tamara, and if you know it means a lot to her . . ."

"Well, what about me? What if I want to spend the weekend with Miguel? Dad only comes once a year, and I want him to meet my boyfriend!" I got up and went into my room. I hated decisions like this. I mean, I was glad Tamara was back, but now that I felt close to Miguel, too, it was harder to share things with her. Not because I didn't trust her, but because I had a boyfriend and she didn't, and I didn't want to make her jealous. Besides, Miguel and I had

180

such close talks, there were things I couldn't share out of loyalty.

On the other hand I knew Tamara was hurt that I wasn't spending more time with her, and I knew she wanted to meet Miguel. When she asked about him yesterday, she seemed almost angry.

"So . . . Leah, when am I going to meet him?"

I shrugged. "He's working most of the weekend."

Tamara's voice grew suspicious. "Yeah, like every weekend. You know, you're worse than Bette. It's a great feeling —coming home and being replaced by the phantom boyfriend. Just tell me, has anyone besides you ever seen him?"

I tried to laugh, but inside I was scared . . . and jealous of Tamara's looks. What if Miguel and Tamara went for each other, I'd lose two people at once. And I couldn't get it out of my mind how all the guys were coming on to her at school—it was much harder to be her friend in certain ways. But the more Tamara bugged me about meeting Miguel, the harder it was for me to think of excuses.

"He can't play guitar and go to church all the time," Tamara teased. "Can't you undo the handcuffs for one Saturday afternoon? You and I don't ever get together outside of school anymore—why can't you arrange something for this weekend or next weekend?

I thought of Dad's invitation for next weekend—how hurt Tamara would be if she found out I was inviting Miguel to Chicago.

"You're being totally weird about this, Leah. You say I'm your best friend, but I've never even met the guy you're supposed to be in love with. It's like you want to keep Miguel hidden or something—he does exist, right? Look, I'll even ask Stewart, my biology partner, if he wants to get together on Saturday, and we can double, okay?"

181

"Do you like Stewart?" I asked.

"He's okay, as a friend."

I knew if I waited any longer she'd really get suspicious, so I told her we'd meet Saturday, after Miguel got off work. I figured the best time to introduce her to Miguel would be then, since Tamara was bringing along someone for herself.

Later, when I told Miguel about my dad's invitation, he hesitated. "I don't know. . . . I mean, it might be hard to get off work, and Grandma might really get suspicious then."

"But I really want you to meet my dad—everyone loves him. Plus, we'll get to see each other for a whole weekend."

Miguel didn't look at me. "It might be weird, though, my being José's nephew and all. I don't know. Anyway, I don't think Sheila will let me off for a whole weekend."

"Ask her, though, okay? And I'll ask José to talk to your grandma."

"Don't say anything to José until I talk to Sheila," he said. "I'll talk to José myself."

Something in his voice made me think that maybe Mom was right. Maybe he didn't want to go.

28

"S tewart should meet us in half an hour, at the pavilion in the park," Tamara told me as we met on the steps outside Century Hall.

"For sure?"

"I think so." Tamara smiled. "I told him yesterday, and he said he'd try to make it."

"Try?" I asked. "What does that mean, Tamara!"

"I told him a group of us were meeting in the park, and if he could come, great. . . . He said he'd try."

Suddenly I knew it was going to be just the three of us. Tamara had set it up just so she could meet Miguel!

"Tamara, did he say he'd be there or not?"

She shrugged. "He said he'd try . . . so what am I supposed to do, hide in the bushes until Stewart comes, then

183

jump out and introduce myself to Miguel as your best friend who's not supposed to show herself unless she's chaperoned? What's the big deal, anyway? Does Miguel look like José or something? Because if that's it, I think José's all right. I mean, I could go for him if I was as ancient as your mom."

I knew Tamara was trying to be funny, but I couldn't laugh. "Miguel's handsome," I whispered.

"So? Then it's me. Okay, so what is it? Am I just too gorgeous or is it my incredibly delightful personality?"

"Tamara, do you always get your way?"

"You know, Leah, you don't have a sense of humor . . . you make such a big deal out of everything. If you want me to leave, just say so."

But I couldn't. Even though I felt used, I couldn't tell her to go. So I just sat there, waiting for Miguel to appear, while Tamara babbled on about Glenview, how all the kids get together in groups and discuss what's happening at home. "One girl has run away nine times since she was eleven."

Part of me was listening, but part of me wasn't. I couldn't stop feeling angry, and I kept looking at Tamara—seeing her the way Miguel would see her when he walked outside. Her hair was loose and wavy, with red tints from the sun. And her eyes were dark, without any mascara. Plus she was wearing the blue jeans that showed off her waist. But what I noticed most was the way she wore her new black wool coat open, with her shirt showing off her body. Her turtleneck definitely emphasized her boobs. That's what Miguel would notice! I mean, she looked like an actress already—it wasn't fair!

"How much longer do we have to wait?" Tamara asked. "Do you always put up with his being late?"

"I don't mind waiting," I stated.

"Leah, you'd wait for a dog if it promised to lick your hand." Tamara laughed. "You're always so nice."

I sat there, stung by her words. I wanted to say something that wasn't nice, something mean, just to show her! That's when I blurted it out, partly out of anger and partly because I was sick of how Tamara always got her way and tried to control me. "Tamara . . ." I paused.

"He obviously doesn't mind keeping us waiting," she interrupted.

"I better tell you before you meet Miguel—I invited him to Chicago next weekend."

She stared at me as though she thought I was joking.

"Dad wanted to meet him," I lied.

I saw the hurt cross her face, though she played it cool, lifting her chin as she spoke. "Oh . . . I wouldn't have been able to go anyway. Mom's taking me shopping for spring clothes."

Still, she wouldn't look me in the eye, and the moment she stopped speaking, I was sorry I'd said anything. I always got a horrible feeling when Tamara turned quiet because words were easy for her, and when she didn't talk, it meant she was really hurt.

There was a long silence before I said, "Miguel will be out soon. Sometimes he gets off a little late." I couldn't figure out why my heart was pounding. Big deal, so Tamara meets Miguel—what's the big worry, I kept telling myself.

"How's it going?" Suddenly Miguel's voice interrupted us, as we both turned to see him standing in the doorway.

"Miguel, this is Tamara. Tamara, this is Miguel." I studied Miguel's face to see if he was attracted to her.

"Hi," Miguel said, smiling. "Sorry I took so long, but

185

Sheila's in one of her moods today, so I had to wait until she was done before I could sweep out the bar."

"No problem." Tamara glanced at me, then Miguel.

"Where's your friend?" Miguel asked Tamara.

"He's supposed to meet us at the bench behind the pavilion," she said. "Let's head over in case he's there already."

It was unbelievably warm for January. We wore our coats open, and Tamara took off her hat. "It must be in the forties," she said.

"No wind," Miguel answered. I kept hoping Miguel would hold my hand or put his arm around me, but he just walked with his arms loose on either side.

"I hear you're an incredible musician," Tamara said. "When do you give your next concert?"

"Whenever I can find an audience." Miguel smiled.

I guess Tamara thought she had to make conversation, because she just kept talking. "Leah says you're like a professional."

"Leah exaggerates." Miguel laughed. "Right now I'm just learning to play the saxophone. It'll make me a more versatile musician if I join a band."

Versatile musician? Where had he heard that one? It sounded like some quote from a music magazine.

"Seriously, I'd like to hear you play sometime," Tamara said. Then, leaning forward so she could see me, she added, "Maybe we could have a party at my place. Bette wouldn't mind as long as she was invited."

"That'd be cool. I could ask some friends of mine who play in a band."

We found a bench and sat down just below the pavilion, Miguel between us. If he didn't do something like at least hold my hand, Tamara would think he didn't really like me.

I listened as Tamara kept talking, nonstop. "Boys get obsessed about things in ways girls don't. Like my brother and basketball, and you with your music." She was talking in a certain way, like she wanted to challenge Miguel.

"Don't girls get obsessed?" Miguel asked, his voice teasing.

"Yeah, about human beings. Girls actually prefer things that breathe."

Miguel laughed, "And boys don't. . . ."

Tamara shook her head, her hair brushing across her shoulders. "Guys need to feel in control. It's genetic. Guitars and basketballs can be placed in closets—and they don't talk back or ask for anything."

"That's true." Miguel punched me lightly in the shoulder. "The guitar is a lot less demanding."

"I mean, my brother Jake," Tamara continued, without letting me say anything, "he's a senior, right? He's never had a girlfriend for like longer than a month, and he admits he doesn't have time because of basketball. Such an exciting guy," she added sarcastically.

"What's he do when he's not playing basketball?"

"He torments me with his presence."

"I know the type." Miguel laughed. "But, hey, I'm an exceptional kind of guy. I have time for my guitar and a girlfriend, right, Leah?"

"Yeah, and probably in that order too." Tamara laughed. "Every guy's an exception in his own mind, wouldn't you say, Leah?"

"True." Miguel grinned. "But I have a witness—Leah will tell you what a wonderful guy I am." He glanced at me. "Your friend obviously doesn't recognize perfection when she sees it."

187

"No, but I recognize an overworked ego." Tamara turned to me. "Do you let him get away with this?"

"With what?" I asked, trying to keep my voice from sounding angry.

Tamara rolled her eyes. "Well, I guess he's got you wrapped around his finger."

My face heated up, and I tried to think of some witty remark to throw back in her face, but my mind went blank when I heard Miguel and Tamara laughing together.

Why was Tamara trying so hard to be funny? She could think of jokes so fast—one-liners—that made me look stupid. It seemed like they were the couple, and I was the new person. I suddenly realized I hadn't said anything. It was their conversation, and they made it impossible for me to say anything!

"Leah said you ran away. . . ." Miguel stated.

"Yeah, I wasn't getting along with my mother."

I had told Miguel most things about Tamara, but I hadn't mentioned her boyfriend in California, mainly because I knew Miguel would find that interesting. He might really like it that Tamara had been wild when she was on her own.

"Did you know anyone out there besides your dad?" Miguel asked.

Tamara glanced at me nervously and shook her head.

"I love California," Miguel stated. "How could you stand to come back?"

I was amazed because Tamara switched the topic and began telling him about Glenview. "The people there are pretty nice, but there are a lot of rules to follow, like not seeing old friends." Tamara smiled at me. "What really helped me out a lot, though, was your uncle talking to my mother. José's fantastic!"

188

"Right, he told me he talked to your mom," Miguel said. "José said she's totally beautiful. I remember her from the Thanksgiving party."

Why hadn't Miguel told me that before!

Tamara nodded. "He talked Bette into a compromise, a brand-new experience for my mother. Bette tends to listen to men, especially if she's attracted to them. She probably has the hots for José."

Great, I thought. Bette gets José, and Tamara gets Miguel. Mom and I can both commit suicide together.

"So it sounds like Glenview takes up most of your free time. Is that why I've never met you before?" Miguel grinned. "Do you ever get to quit?"

My whole chest was paralyzed, my body was about to crumble into tears. I knew what he was asking. I could translate. Why didn't he just come right out and say it— *When are you available?*

Tamara glanced at me quickly. "Leah never invites me anymore—there's this rumor that she's got a boyfriend, this guy."

I couldn't believe Tamara would say that . . . making me look bad.

"Yeah." Miguel laughed. "I've heard the rumor . . . he's supposed to be a handsome, brilliant musician."

"God, she must have two boyfriends, then!" Tamara thought she had to be the comedian, but I was sick of being the subject of her jokes.

"So do you miss California?" Miguel asked. "Did you meet some interesting people?"

"She met too many interesting people!" I laughed.

Tamara stopped smiling as the tone of the conversation changed. She and I both knew I'd introduced a subject that wasn't mine to bring up. We looked at each other, both of us

189

feeling the tension. . . . I could see Tamara's face turn red as she looked away. I couldn't tell if her eyes were wincing or squinting, but she definitely wasn't happy.

"Things didn't work out the way she thought, right Tamara?" I smiled at her. For once there was a balance in the conversation, and now maybe she wouldn't try to be funny all the time.

"So how is it being home?" Miguel asked her.

She stared at me, but spoke to him. "People change, even in a few weeks. The things you think you can count on don't last . . . like promises between best friends."

At first Miguel thought she was just joking around some more. "Yeah, life's rough," he added, teasing her. "Leah's changed, thanks to my positive influence."

"Exactly." Tamara's voice turned cold. "Two's company, three's—"

"Three's fine with me." Miguel laughed. "As long as I'm the only guy."

"Tamara, we've both changed, you and me," I added quickly.

"I'm the one who always phones you, Leah, and half the time your line's busy because you're always talking to Miguel."

"I don't call you because Bette hates me."

Tamara rolled her eyes. "Sure."

"Should I leave?" Miguel looked nervous as he stared at me.

Tamara ignored Miguel momentarily. "You've been telling me about your dad ever since we met. In a way I felt like he was the perfect father, you know? It may not be a big deal to you, but I'd been looking forward to meeting him, and you promised me . . . a long time ago. You prom-

190

ised!" For the first time Tamara's eyes had tears in them, and her voice clouded over.

"Tamara, you've changed too."

The moment I spoke, I regretted my words. I could see it, the shadow crossing her face. I'd seen it when she was with Bette, getting ready to say something mean.

Tamara turned to Miguel. "You can't imagine how much we've both changed. I don't lie anymore"—she laughed—"and Leah doesn't dislike Mexicans."

"Tamara," I yelled, "I never said that!"

"Why don't you tell Miguel what you used to say about José!"

"I never said anything about him being Mexican!"

"No, but you talked about the way he greases his hair back and wears shiny shirts—you said you could see why he wasn't hired as the principal!"

"Tamara—you're lying!"

"And the only reason you didn't want me to meet Miguel is because you're embarrassed of the way he dresses! You're always complaining about his tight pants and his leather jacket." Tamara looked down at Miguel's shoes. "And those sleazy shoes."

"Tamara, shut up!" I screamed. "Shut up your stupid lies!"

I turned to Miguel, who was staring at me. "She's lying," I whispered. "She always lies about everything!"

"If you think I'm lying, ask José about the time Leah borrowed my mother's clothes and tried to seduce him. She wanted to ruin their relationship, right, Leah?" Tamara smiled. "She was scared she might end up having Mr. Margarita as a stepfather!"

Then she turned and laughed. "Obviously Stewart isn't coming. It's been great meeting you, Miguel. Have a great

191

time in Chicago next weekend. Leah must really like you to have changed so much." Then, without looking at me, Tamara turned and walked off.

Just when she was about to turn the corner, beyond the pavilion, I yelled out, "No wonder your mom wants to send you away."

Then I saw Miguel's eyes, full of doubt as he searched my face.

We stood there silently. "Miguel . . ." I whispered, grabbing his hand.

But he shrugged me off. He was too angry to let me speak and too hurt to speak himself. We sat there for a few seconds, until finally he whispered, "Why didn't you introduce me to her before?"

I hesitated. "Because I thought you'd go for her, like today!"

"I don't even know her!" Miguel replied.

"But you'd have a much better chance with her than me, right? She's a freer sort of person. . . ."

"You think that's all I care about?"

"She's so beautiful . . . and I thought you might like her, really like her." I started crying. "And you never even touched me this whole afternoon!"

"Well, sorry I didn't perform for your friend!" He stood up and started walking away, then turned in my direction. "What'd you expect me to do? Make out with you while she watches?"

"Miguel, you know that what Tamara said this afternoon wasn't true . . . she lies all the time."

He looked at me. "I don't know what I know."

"Miguel, when Mom met José, I was jealous of her—it was like I'd lost my father and I was suddenly losing my mother too. Part of what Tamara said was true, I said bad

192

things about José, but I would have hated any man. And I really like José now. I want Mom to marry him."

Tears streamed down my face, but I kept talking, trying to make Miguel understand. "What Tamara said about you wasn't true. I didn't introduce her to you because I was jealous—I knew Tamara would go for you, and I thought you'd maybe like her better, so I didn't want you to meet her."

"She'd never go for me. I'm not her type—she's too classy!"

His words formed a fist that seemed to punch me in slow motion. There was no air, nothing to breathe in. *If she's so classy, then what am I?*

I looked at Miguel, who stood a few feet away, staring over the bluffs toward Lake Michigan. I felt the same ache I'd felt all year—the moments of distance after moments of closeness. Nothing stays the same, I realized, nothing. Not Tamara. Not Miguel. And I'd changed, too, only sometimes the changes seemed out of control.

Mom once told me that people who are close hear each other's feelings, not each other's words. Only right now, all I heard were Miguel's and Tamara's words. It seemed as if I had no voice of my own, nothing inside that belonged to me.

Miguel sat down on the bench next to me and stared out at the water—there was a freight barge moving slowly across the horizon.

"I think maybe we should see each other less for a while," he whispered. "Maybe—"

Panic filled me. "Because of today, what Tamara said?" I interrupted.

"Not because of today." He paused. "It's like things are starting to get too complicated. When we first met, it was

193

simple—I liked you and you liked me, and we saw each other when we could. Then there was the fight between José and your mom, and that started me thinking about how different our families are—how different you are from me." "But that doesn't matter," I told him. "We're alike in a lot of ways too."

"And then with your dad's invitation, you didn't really give me a choice whether I wanted to go. And today, the fight between you and Tamara." Miguel smiled sadly. "It's not simple anymore."

I froze—was he saying he didn't want a girlfriend?

"I like calling you and talking," he added, "and I like seeing you weekends." His voice was gentle, like a feather running up my spine. "But sometimes routines get in the way of things you really want, like next weekend. There's a band at Century Hall that I want to see, and anyway, I'm not ready to meet your dad and go through the whole boyfriend scene. I don't want to have to prove myself to anyone."

"My dad's not like that."

Miguel looked at me. "Leah, it doesn't matter. I'm not ready to spend a weekend with your father."

"We wouldn't be with them the whole time," I whispered. "We'd be together."

"I guess what I mean is that there are other things that mean a lot to me, too, and I don't think I can do those things and be someone's boyfriend all the time, so it's probably better if we're just friends."

"Couldn't we try just being close on weekends or something?" An urgency was starting to fill up inside me. I didn't want to lose him. "Maybe if we just saw each other less?"

Miguel smiled but said nothing.

194

"Would it be different if I were closer to you . . . physically? I mean, I'm starting to feel that maybe. . . ."

He shook his head and pulled me closer.

"But what about your Christmas present? You signed it love." I sat up and moved away from him. "Miguel why are you changing? I don't understand how anyone can change so fast."

"Leah, I haven't changed that much. I don't want to stop seeing you. I just don't want to be tied down." He paused and looked at his watch. "We'll have to wait and talk about it later. I'm supposed to be back at work right now."

I sat, unable to say anything. I wanted him to hug me and hold me close.

"I've got to take off." He squeezed my arm. "I'm already late."

I nodded, trying to hold back the tears.

"Take it easy, okay? I'll meet you after work and we can talk about it then, all right? I'll be off at eight."

I knew he was trying to make it easier. Only, his words were just words. They didn't come close to touching my feelings. From the bench I watched him walk away, growing smaller in the distance, while the emptiness grew larger inside. I kept remembering the day Mom caught us kissing—afterward she'd told José that people don't need a reason to like each other, but they need a reason to stay together. And I wondered, when Miguel turned the corner without looking back, if I could prove to him there was a reason for us to stay together.

195

29

Miguel never even called to tell me he'd be late, so I stood outside the drugstore where we were supposed to meet until almost nine o'clock, an hour later than we'd planned. First I worried that maybe he had been in some kind of accident. Then I started thinking maybe he was mad about our talk earlier in the day, and he was going to dump me without ever seeing me again. Just when I was about to call Mrs. Santiago and disguise my voice so I could find out where Miguel was, he came walking down the sidewalk with Jonathan, laughing and talking like being late was no big deal.

"So you waited. . . ." he said, as the two of them got close. "Sheila told me to help the band set up. It was great. I got to talk to the lead guitarist about their gigs and how they go about finding bars to play in."

I stared at Miguel, who was talking more to Jonathan than me. Wasn't he even going to say he was sorry?

"How long they gonna be playin' there?" Jonathan asked, pulling out a pack of cigarettes. He put the cigarette in his mouth so that it hung out the corner while he talked. Personally, I didn't know what Miguel saw in him, except that Jonathan had taught him how to play the saxophone.

Miguel's voice got excited. "Chris, he manages the band. He told me he goes around to all the bars and gives sample tapes to the managers. He told me he could introduce me to some of the bar owners." Miguel paused. "At first they were playing for a hundred and fifty a night, split five ways. Now they're playing for six hundred. Took them just over a year."

Whenever Miguel gets around one of the guys from work, he stands in a certain way, his legs spread, one slightly in front of the other, shoulders back, so his chest stretches wide and his leather jacket hangs open. If I didn't know him, I'd think he was tough, but that's because when he's with the guys, his face doesn't show much emotion.

"Hey, sounds all right to me, man." Jonathan zipped up his coat. "Take it easy." Then he flicked his cigarette beyond the curb and walked down the street, his shoulders swaying side to side.

"Good dude," Miguel said as he watched Jonathan turn the corner. "He swept up for me tonight, so I could talk to the band longer."

I stood there, glaring at Miguel. My voice came out sarcastic, "Yeah, good dude!" so that Miguel knew I thought he sounded stupid.

"So?" I asked, my eyes opening wider.

197

"So," Miguel repeated, "you shouldn't have waited. You shouldn't be out here by yourself."

My mouth hung open. "What! I was waiting so we could talk about this afternoon!"

"Sometimes things come up at work."

"What kind of things come up at work?" I asked angrily. "Do you always do whatever Sheila asks? Like a good boy?"

Miguel's face turned red. "Look, when Sheila asked me to help out tonight, there wasn't any time to call you. I knew you'd have left already. The band got there late, so I had to fill in. It was a great opportunity to make some contacts."

Was this what he meant by no routines? Like there was nothing wrong with being an hour late, as long as he had an excuse?

I stood there, my chin trembling. I felt so angry, and at the same time, so scared. I didn't want to nag him. Dad once told me there's nothing that turns men off more than a woman who nags. At the same time I felt as if Miguel didn't really care about my feelings. It hurt to think that all afternoon, I'd been worrying about us, and he'd been talking to some stupid musicians about their band.

"Okay, sorry." Miguel glanced at his watch. "So what do you want to do now?"

I shrugged. "I don't care." I was looking everywhere but at him.

"Well, to tell you the truth, I'm kind of tired." Miguel paused and glanced around. "Maybe I'll just ride you home on the bus, and we can call it a night. I wouldn't mind practicing my sax a little."

When we got on the bus, I had to concentrate my whole mind on not crying. I kept taking deep breaths as I sat by

198

the window staring at the streetlights go by. No way was I going to talk to him. No way. But even as I sat there, thinking all the bad thoughts I could about him, my breath caught and began to chip away inside my chest, until all the thoughts turned hard inside me and took my breath away, like being held underwater. He was holding me down. His silence.

His arm went around my shoulder, but I still didn't look at him. I felt him lean toward me, his face close to mine.

"You're quiet," he whispered.

I nodded, without turning toward him.

"You mad?"

I kept nodding.

"Because I was late?"

I shrugged. "Not just that."

"Then what?" Miguel let out a long, impatient sigh. "Are you mad because of what I told you earlier?"

"When you're around your friends, you're different. You close me off. You act like we're not close, and you don't seem to care at all how I feel."

"That's not true. I asked you what you wanted to do tonight, and you said you didn't care."

"Then you said you'd rather practice your sax than be with me."

"That's not what I said. I'm tired, and I could tell right away you were in a bitchy mood, so I thought maybe it'd be better if we did our own thing tonight, you know?"

"Yeah, everything was fine until today." Tears started streaming down my cheeks and my nose started to run. "You wouldn't have suggested we do our own thing a month ago." I opened my purse and pulled out a Kleenex.

"Come on," Miguel whispered. "At least wait until we

199

get to your house." His tone softened, and his arm tightened around my shoulder, pulling me closer to him. But I jerked away. Inside there was an ache, the kind of ache that comes in a dream when you begin to fall. In my dreams I'm always falling from the top step, away from the people I care about most.

I knew things could end. I'd seen it happen lots of times. People could change and never feel the same about each other—I'd seen it with Mom and Dad, and with Tamara's parents too. The more I cared about Miguel, the more his feelings seemed to change. There was a hole inside me, the place in me that needed him. It was deep. I suddenly felt like I could fall into that hole, and keep falling—and he might not even notice!

When we got off the bus, Miguel took my hand and held it tightly. I still couldn't look at him, not without crying. He moved close and hugged me, then his lips kissed my forehead and my lips. "What's up?" he whispered, his breath warming my ear. I hugged him tighter so he couldn't see my face. I was afraid to have him see me. Afraid he'd see how much I cared.

"Hey," Miguel whispered, his voice all air. "Talk."

"I don't want anything to change." I sobbed. "But you're changing. I can feel it."

Miguel hugged me. There was a long pause before he spoke. "Leah, I can't help it. Music is really important to me, and I don't want to have to worry about being late, like tonight, and hurting you."

I knew he was going to start talking about music again, and I wanted to keep him talking about us—so I kissed him, hard. I wanted him to love me so much, more than music and everything else.

It was ten o'clock when we reached my house. José and

200

Mom were out, and Mom had said they wouldn't be in until after midnight.

"Miguel," I wrapped my arms around him and whispered, "I want you to love me." I pulled him over to the couch next to me. "I can change too. I want to change."

His eyes turned soft. "Leah, we need to talk some more."

"I don't want to talk."

I wanted to show him that I cared about him, that what Tamara had said earlier wasn't true. I wanted to prove to him that our relationship was more important than everything. I pulled him close, and kissed him again. "You said you didn't want a routine," I whispered. "That would be okay with me. Couldn't we still be together sometimes?"

Miguel sat back, apart from me. "Leah, I just want us to be friends."

"But why?" I couldn't hold back the sobs. "Why does everything have to change?"

He pulled me close and held me for a long time, until I stopped crying. Then he squeezed my hand and stood up.

"I have to catch my bus—it's almost midnight."

I felt his arms hug me tight. My body wanted to surround him, crawl inside his touch and stay there, get as much as I could of him to last . . . but the minute he was gone, with the door closed and the house silent, I had only one thought—I was all alone again.

30

When I heard the doorbell ring at eight in the morning, I woke hoping it would be Miguel—that he had changed his mind.

José grinned as I walked into the kitchen in my bathrobe and slippers. "We want you to be the first to know."

"Know what?" I rubbed my eyes, still swollen from last night's crying.

José grinned as he pulled a bottle of champagne from behind his back and popped the cork. "As soon as your mom graduates, we're getting married."

Of all the days to announce their decision, they'd chosen this, the worst.

"Congratulations," I said, my chin quivering as I tried to control my tears.

Mom and José looked at each other, surprised. "What's up?" Mom asked. "We thought you'd be happy."

"I'm happy for you," I mumbled. "It's just that . . ."

"What?"

The tears rolled down my cheeks. "Miguel and I . . . it's over."

"So that's why Tamara called twice last night and said she had to talk to you?" Mom asked.

"No." I shook my head, crying even harder. "Tamara and I had a huge fight yesterday."

As Mom put her arms around me, she turned to José. "Better call Miguel and tell him not to come over this morning."

"He's coming here?"

José nodded. "We thought we'd have a champagne breakfast to celebrate."

"But we'll call it off," Mom whispered. "We can do it another time."

"No . . . that would be worse. I don't want him feeling sorry for me because he thinks I can't handle it."

Just then the phone rang.

"I'm sure it's Tamara—when she called last night, she said it was urgent."

I shook my head, "Tell her I'm not here. I'm never going to be here again when she calls."

When Mom picked up the receiver, she looked surprised. "Hi, Miguel. Yes, she's right here."

I pulled the phone into my room and closed the door.

"Hi," he said.

"Hi."

"I just wanted to call and see if you're okay. You heard the news, right? About your mom and José?"

"Yeah. . . ."

203

"José asked me to come over and celebrate at your house, but I wanted to see if that was okay with you . . . after last night and everything. I didn't tell him about us because I didn't want to spoil his news. But I wanted to make sure it's okay with you if I come."

"It's okay."

"You sure?"

There was a long pause as I tried to keep from getting choked up.

"Leah," he said gently, "are you okay?"

"Yeah."

"We're practically family now."

That made me feel even worse, and I couldn't answer, not without crying.

"You're sure it's okay if I come over this morning?"

I took a deep breath. "I'm sure."

"I'll see you in a little while, then."

After I hung up, I felt the ache inside open up. Mom came into my room and I told her, "Miguel wants to be friends, but I know whenever I see him, I'm going to feel like crying."

"Does he still want to see you?" Mom asked.

"I guess so, but it's like suddenly we can't touch each other. And I'm not going to be able to tell him how I really feel."

Mom nodded and hugged me close.

A few seconds later the doorbell rang. The moment I heard it, I knew it was Tamara. Nobody else would arrive this early on a Sunday morning without calling first. But I wasn't ready to see her, not when I was so mixed up about things with Miguel. Tamara would be glad he'd split up with me. It's exactly what she'd wanted, and it would be one more time that she had won and had gotten her way.

204

"It's Tamara," I told Mom. "Tell her I'm not here."

"You tell her," Mom whispered.

"What am I supposed to say?" I asked angrily. "I don't have anything to say to her! Just tell her I went to Chicago or something—anything! I don't want to see her, especially this morning, after what happened with Miguel."

Mom waved her hand at me to get out of the hallway and opened the front door.

"Hi, Mrs. Lucas." I heard Tamara's voice. "I need to talk to Leah."

"She's not here, Tamara. Can I give her a message?"

Tamara's voice rose and wavered as though she were about to cry. "I know she's in there. I heard her voice—I know she's mad, but all I want to do is say I'm sorry. Couldn't you just tell her that and see if she'll come talk to me?"

I heard Mom mumble something. Then she peeked into my room. "She knows you're home. She just wants to apologize. Leah, you might as well talk it out now. Otherwise it'll keep bothering you."

"There's nothing to talk out, Mom. She's the one who ruined my relationship with Miguel. She turned him against me."

"Leah, I'm going to let her come in."

"No!" I stood up reluctantly. I didn't want Miguel arriving with Tamara in the house. Then he'd really suspect that I'd lied to him—in a way I felt I had to be angry for both of us, for the way she hurt me, and him.

"Go talk to her," Mom whispered.

As soon as I opened the front door, Tamara spoke fast. "I'm sorry, Leah."

I stood there, feeling a rush of anger. It was just

205

like Tamara to barge in anytime she wanted, without calling first.

"Could we go for a walk and talk?"

"Mom?" I yelled. "How long until breakfast?" I was hoping she'd say five minutes.

"José has to run to the store, so it'll be at least an hour."

"Just a minute," I told Tamara. I ran into my room and got dressed, then grabbed my coat and scarf.

Outside, I walked next to Tamara, without saying anything.

"So are you going to stay mad or what?" she asked.

"Yes."

"I said I was sorry."

"It doesn't matter what you say," I told her. "Why should I trust you?"

Up the block was an old churchyard where we sat down on the wrought-iron bench. "Come on, Leah. Don't stay mad. I'll write *I'm sorry* a thousand times on a piece of paper." Tamara giggled. "I'll tattoo it on my forehead, all right? Will that be enough proof?"

Hearing Tamara laugh made me even angrier. "Tamara, I was never embarrassed about Miguel's pants and jacket. I never said anything about his clothes, so why'd you say that?"

There was a long pause. "You talked about José's clothes."

"But I never said one thing to you about the way Miguel dressed."

"I was angry."

"So that gave you the right to lie?"

"You lied too." Tamara's voice rose.

"When?"

"You didn't tell me before that you were inviting Miguel

206

to Chicago. You let me think I was going to be invited to meet your dad."

"That's not the same!" My voice rose, and suddenly I heard myself yelling. "You always turn things around, Tamara, just to blame other people!"

Tamara shouted back, "It is too the same. Your silence is worse than lying. You didn't tell me the truth about asking Miguel, so I thought I was invited. I was really excited. It would have been better to lie and tell me you were going by yourself or something." Tamara stared at me. "Proof is proof!"

"Proof of what?" I didn't like the way she was trying to make it look like the fight was my fault.

"Proof that you replaced me really fast." Tamara's eyes had tears in them. "You're just like everyone else. I was stupid to think that maybe we were really best friends."

"Tamara, you were the one who left. You were the one who lied! You're the one who kept silent on the phone and made me feel lousy. It was easy to be best friends before you ran away, but when you came back, you constantly tried to make me feel guilty because I finally had a boyfriend."

"But you changed so much!" Tamara wiped a tear from her face. "You never made time for me—I always had to fit into the time slots when Miguel couldn't see you."

"That's not true," I yelled. "Anyway, when you used to talk about guys, I was never mean to you, even when I was jealous."

She stared at me. "You were jealous?"

"Yeah, but even when I felt that way, I didn't try to hurt you." I looked away, toward the street. "You'll be pleased to hear that Miguel doesn't want to be my boyfriend anymore—thanks to you!"

"Leah, you're just saying that."

207

"It's true."

"I'm sorry," Tamara whispered. "I'm really sorry."

But I hated her at that moment, hated the way she always felt sorry afterward—after getting her way. "It didn't matter that you hurt me, but you hurt Miguel. You made it sound like I always made fun of him behind his back." Suddenly my voice rose, and I was yelling, louder than before. "I don't care if you're sorry, Tamara—it doesn't matter now!"

Tamara sat up and looked down the street, opposite me. "Leah, everybody lies sometimes."

"Maybe, but there are limits, you know? I don't tell lies to hurt people, like you do."

"Yeah, even your lies are better than mine."

"What's that supposed to mean, Tamara?"

"The truth is, Leah, you lie all the time by keeping your mouth shut!" Tamara smiled. "At least I have the courage to say what I think!"

"It takes a lot of courage to hurt people, doesn't it, Tamara?"

"Come on, Leah, I said I was sorry—can't we just forget it?"

"No!"

"So how long are you going to stay mad at me?"

I shrugged.

She grinned again. "I mean, who else recognizes a three-alarm chili? And turkey vegetable? Who else gets bored in tedious, Rachel-type situations?"

Tamara was laughing as she talked, but I couldn't laugh.

"Look, Leah, lighten up. I may have said stupid things, but ever since we met, you've always been my best friend."

I felt so confused, listening to Tamara try to make ev-

208

erything okay—only, it wasn't okay. This time I felt too angry and sad to giggle with her, and at the same time I missed the way it used to be between us, when we laughed until our stomachs ached. I wanted to laugh like that again, but I couldn't.

"Want to go to the Mall this afternoon? We could follow guys."

"No."

"Leah?" Tamara said in a hoarse voice. "Remember how you hated José at first because your mom loved him? That's how I felt the minute I met Miguel. I saw why you liked him more and I wanted to flirt with him just to make you mad, and then when you got mad at me instead of him, I wanted to do something to ruin things. . . ."

"Mom and José are getting married."

"So maybe Miguel will change his mind before the wedding," Tamara whispered. "I'll call him and admit I lied if that would make him see—"

Suddenly I couldn't stand it, couldn't stand Tamara's suggestions, the way she always tried to take charge. "No . . . it's too late," I screamed at her. "It's too late, and it's your fault. For once you can't just fix things—and make everything fall into place your way!" I got up and started to leave.

"Leah, wait!" Tamara ran up next to me and grabbed my mitten. "Leah, you can't just cut me off like this. I mean, I know everything about you, and you know everything about me. Who are you going to talk to now? Your mom's got José, and Miguel's gone. So I'm it—I'm what's left." Tamara started giggling. "And who else will share lipstick with you?"

I realized then that Tamara would always make real feelings into a joke, it was her way.

"And I don't wear pointy shoes that could stab your ankle if we walk close." She giggled. "You're definitely safer with me."

Suddenly, the hurt of being with Tamara seemed much larger than all the laughter we'd shared. We were close, all right, but it wasn't a closeness that felt safe anymore.

"I'll see you at school," I told her, and turned to walk up the sidewalk.

"Leah, what's that supposed to mean?" She ran up next to me. "Aren't we going to talk before school? Can't I call you tonight?" Tamara started laughing again, only this time, she stopped as soon as she saw that I was crying.

"Leah, what did I say wrong this time?"

"You never mean to say anything that hurts, but you do —that's why I can't talk to you anymore, Tamara." I turned and ran from her, around the house, toward the back door.

"Will you talk to me . . . at school?" Tamara called after me.

But I was crying too hard to answer. There was no language that said good-bye the way it felt, nothing that could make it hurt less.

I crouched under the kitchen window and listened to Miguel's voice inside. José had opened the window to let out some smoke from burning toast—I could smell the burning bread along with smells of bacon and coffee.

"I'm going to work more hours and then take off time in the summer for the music institute," Miguel was telling Mom.

"You'll sing at the wedding, won't you?"

"Sure."

"Will Sheila let you off for a month," José asked, "for music classes?"

"Yeah, Jonathan will take my hours."

I sat there listening—they were discussing music, discussing the wedding!

"Breakfast is ready," José announced.

"Let's wait for Leah," Mom said. "I told her an hour."

"It's been an hour and a half," José said. "Maybe she and Tamara went off somewhere."

"Want me to walk around the block and look for them?" Miguel asked.

"Please, and if you see her," Mom told him, "just ask her if she wants us to wait."

I didn't want them to wait. I didn't want to see them. I sneaked around the front of the house and ran fast, before Miguel had time to get his coat and come outside. I couldn't be with them—not when they were discussing weddings and music. What about my life!

I hurried along the icy sidewalk and crossed the street. "Leah!"

Looking back, I saw Miguel yelling to me.

"Leah, wait up."

Only, there was nothing to wait for. I didn't want to ruin their happiness, but I couldn't be happy for them, not then, not as alone as I felt. I kept walking fast and heard the front door slam shut, so I knew he'd gone back inside for Mom.

I could explain to Mom later—explain the pain. It hurt to lose people. I could still hear Tamara's voice apologizing, but I knew that even though we might remain friends at school, I would never be able to tell her everything—like I did before. She'd turned my secrets against me, and though I knew she was sorry, I also knew it could happen again. Tamara's stories were part of her, part of what I loved most about her—and hated too.

211

I walked along the shoreline in the bitter cold wind until my feet were numb. I felt the wind breathe through me, through my coat and sweater, against my skin. At the edge of the park I stopped and turned around.

I felt the last two days had equaled all the other years of my life—so many changes. Even the apartment where Mom and I had lived for five years seemed less my own. As though her decision to get married had been a private, separate decision, and it made her life seem less connected to mine.

Forty-eight hours ago I'd thought closeness was all that mattered. I'd always believed that if I was really nice and gave a lot of myself to someone, I'd get the same back. I hadn't realized there were different kinds of closeness—closeness that connected people, like with Mom and José, and the other side of closeness, that smothered people or was used against them.

I walked back up the hill overlooking the lake, and as I turned the corner, I saw Mom and José looking out the window. Mom came outside and leaned against the car and watched me—without waving, without smiling—as though for the first time she was waiting for me to make the first move, waiting to see what I needed.

José came to the window and looked out at Mom. He picked up his coat, but she shook her head. She didn't want him to come outside. Seeing them smile at each other, I felt another kind of ache, because I realized that they were starting their life together, and I was starting my life alone. Part of me wanted to turn around and run away, away from their wedding, with Miguel singing at it, and away from all their plans for the future. But there was no place else to go.

I didn't want Mom to come after me. Nor did I want José to pat me on the back and tell me everything would work out. I didn't want Miguel to talk about his music as though we'd never been close. And most of all, I didn't want Tamara to meet me at my locker on Monday and joke about our fight.

I didn't want any of them to expect me to be the same.

The sound of the lake carried as water pounded the rocks below, drowning all other sounds, even my own tears turning to ice on the inside of my scarf. I wasn't crying just because I was sad. I was crying because I'd never felt so close to my own life, the things I liked and didn't like about myself. The feelings inside weren't happy, or easy to sort through, but they felt right because they made me realize how I was changing. Before, I'd always seen everyone else around me change, especially Tamara and Miguel. I'd felt left out, as though their lives were disconnected from mine.

It was different now—I didn't feel the need to rush home and escape into my room. And I didn't have to spend all my time waiting for Miguel's or Tamara's phone calls either. There was a strange sort of relief in knowing that I was changing too.

I looked at Mom—for once, she wasn't coming after me, pretending to know what I was feeling or what I needed.

And I didn't have to pretend either.

Before I turned back toward her and crossed the street, I took a deep breath and looked at the shimmering water. The lake changed too, moment to moment. I had always liked it that no one could see to the other side—that it kept me wondering what was out there, beyond my view.

About the Author

CAROL DINES was born in Rochester, Minnesota, in 1956. After receiving her B.A. from Stanford University and her M.A. in creative writing from Colorado State University, she taught at universities in Minnesota, Wisconsin, and Florida. She has published poetry in various journals, and *Best Friends Tell the Best Lies,* which won a Wisconsin Arts Board grant, is her first novel for Delacorte. She is currently the co-director of the Writers-in-the-Schools program in Gainesville, Florida, where she resides with her husband and daughter.